THE
Stamp Collector

David Benedictus

WEIDENFELD & NICOLSON

LONDON

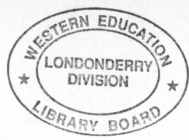

First published in Great Britain in 1994 by
Weidenfeld & Nicolson

The Orion Publishing Group Ltd
Orion House
5 Upper Saint Martin's Lane
London WC2H 9EA

A catalogue record for this book is available from the British
Library

ISBN 0 297 81350 1

Typeset at The Spartan Press Ltd, Lymington, Hants
Printed in Great Britain by Butler & Tanner Ltd,
Frome & London

Grateful acknowledgement is made for use of extracts
from the following songs:

'Gal in Calico' (Arthur Schwartz, Leo Robin)
© 1946, Remick Music Corp., USA
Reproduced by permission of B. Feldman and Co. Ltd,
London WC2H 0EA
(For the British Commonwealth, Republic of Ireland
and South Africa)
© 1946 WARNER BROS. INC. (Renewed)
All rights reserved. Used by permission.
(For Australasia and Canada)

'I Thought About You' (Johnny Mercer)
© Warner Chappell Music Limited, London
Reproduced by permission of International Music
Publications Limited.

To Several People with love and thanks.
And thanks specifically to Edmund Rick for technical advice.

Part One

1

'*I* need to know – am I dying?'

'We all are, Mr Marshall.'

'You're a fool. I'm surrounded by fools.'

'I can assure you that in this clinic –'

'You are about to tell me that in this clinic you don't admit fools?'

'I can assure you –'

'It's the remark of a fool.'

'I have been in the business long enough to know that the patient is always right.'

'All your patients?'

'Every one.'

'I have been a patient long enough to know that that's nonsense.'

Dr Zilkha smiled ingratiatingly: 'You're right of course, sir.'

'Huh!'

Bertram Marshall would have welcomed the opportunity of criticising the clinic. If he was dying, he would have liked the opportunity of blaming it on inefficiency. But if the clinic was all that it appeared to be – and it appeared to be as luxurious and impersonal as the latest addition to a chain of international hotels – then he was dying of mortality and his removal to another clinic would not cure that.

'How long do you give me, if give isn't an inappropriate word in a place like this?'

Dr Zilkha, an immaculately presented Arab with brown eyes of such sweetness that one might have believed that to look at them was to be cured of all ills, glanced at his Rolex as if it were a matter of hours, as if the clinic was so efficient that he could say, By teatime, or by twenty-one hundred hours and so it would be, with the inevitability of an impeccably run institution. But he merely replied:

'Perhaps weeks, possibly months, and it could even be years, though the body is slowing down.'

Unimpressed by soft, brown eyes, for he was no stranger to a treacherous world, Marshall snorted.

'What am I to make of that? If I ring up a builder and say: Is my house falling down? and the builder says: Perhaps weeks, possibly months, and it could even be years, I employ another builder.'

'Your body is more complicated than a house. We can measure your heartbeat and the pressure of your blood; we can listen to your lungs and test your reflexes; but there remains an invisible –'

'Invisible rats!' snarled Marshall. 'Tell me something I don't know. If there is anything you know and I don't.'

'Very well. We have identified a new tumour lodged behind your heart. My colleagues and I do not believe that it is operable. At the moment it is quite small. About the size of a plover's egg. Clearly visible.'

Marshall managed a smile. 'A small thing, but mine own.' What he had just heard was like a precious stamp he had just acquired; he put it to one side to be examined later.

'So the house is falling down,' he said. 'One might have expected it to stand a little longer.'

Houses he had known. The one he had known best.

2

*I*t was shaded from the sun by a cluster of firs. On the brightest day the lawn was speckled with light and dotted with needles. The needles were a hazard to a crawling child. He remembered being discouraged by them when tiny. Later, he was to find them a hazard on the bumpy grass tennis court. Around the lawn clusters of rhododendrons. Huge and regular blooms which, to his childish imagination, had appeared like watchers in the bushes, with big silly faces. Visitors to the house used to remark on the rhododendron bushes, praising them for their size, proliferation and brilliance. As a child Marshall despised such remarks – why did they always comment on the obvious?

These were important visitors. Marshall assumed that all visitors were. Liveried chauffeurs brought them in glistening cars. On the coffin-shaped bonnets of the cars the shadows of the firs hung like mourners around a grave. Black and grey were the colours of the cars and the chauffeurs, the firs and the shadows; only the women dared to essay a splash of yellow, a dart of pink. The visitors would climb stiffly out of their cars, bark orders to their chauffeurs, and then when they met their host and hostess it was for a while all rhododendrons.

In those days servants would wait at table, and bring dishes from the kitchen covered with vast silver-plated hoods. Placed in front of his mother, the dishes would wait, the cynosure of hungry eyes, until Lady Marshall grasped the plaited handle and exposed a turkey, a duck, two pheasants, six pigeons, a saddle of lamb, a salmon with a lemon in its mouth and vertebrae of cucumber and tomato slices. From that moment rhododendrons would be dropped from the conversation to be replaced by turkeys, ducks, pheasants, pigeons, lamb or salmon.

'Pot luck!' she would say with an engaging laugh, and everyone laughed too because lies are so much more amusing than the truth.

Bertram was frustrated not to hear these powerful and important visitors discoursing on whatever it was they had come down to Tall Trees to discuss. Clearly they had not motored all the way from the capital to talk of flowers and food. Had that been so, why all these battered but important-looking cases, and those lengthy sessions closeted in the study? If the weather was clement, Alison, Lady Marshall, would take the wives on a tour of the garden and introduce them to the delights of the gazebo, the hammock under the oak tree, the mulberry with its decadent benison of slug-like fruit, the En-Tout-Cas tennis court, the pool with its sheen of water-boatmen and dying insects, the family of foxes in the bracken. But Sir James would be engaged in the business of the day, from which Bertram was excluded. He could tag along with the women – but why should he? – he could keep his own company up-stairs, or he could hover in the corridor, sliding on the rugs, making faces in the glass of the display cabinets, alert to raised voices and carelessly open doors, vulnerable to officious servants.

'Why are you always hovering?' they would ask.

'I've got to be *somewhere*.'

Other people had places where they fitted in. Bertram's

landscapes were always foreign. Even his bedroom. Even his bed.

Sylvia was born when Marshall was eight.

3

'Gawd help us!' exclaimed Sylvia, shocked at the
lavishness of the hospital. Her peculiar brand of puritanism
insisted that to spend money on the sick and dying was the
worst kind of extravagance. To spend it on the healthy was
only marginally better. 'There was even a security man on the
door. Are they afraid the patients will make a break for it?
What's this place cost you, Marshall?'

'Three hundred a night. Except the Private Patients Plan
pays.'

'I'll nurse you for half that,' muttered his sister.

'But you're not registered with the PPP.'

'Three hundred a night. Where's the registrar?' Sylvia
chortled with the sound of water leaving a bath, then
recovered herself. 'What's the prognosis?'

'Perhaps weeks, possibly months, and it could even be
years.'

'That what you pay three hundred a night for?'

'They've a vested interest in keeping me going.'

'I shall miss you, Marshall. When you've only got one
remaining relative . . .'

'You've got your children.'

Sylvia seemed surprised: 'Oh them. Yes, I have, haven't I?
They're quite good news. Them.'

Marshall regarded her with fraternal animosity. 'You have the most appalling dress sense of anyone I've ever met. What is that you've got on? It looks like something bought second-hand in the kasbah.'

Sylvia seemed delighted. 'It was reduced from eighty-five to fifteen. How could I not buy it?'

'To buy it is one thing. What's unforgivable is to wear it.'

'Jack likes it.'

'Well, precisely. He probably likes James Last. And the Battersea Power Station. I'm surprised he hasn't asked you to wear that.'

A nurse came in dressed in the manner of an airline stewardess of the Sixties. She carried a leather-bound folder, containing the day's menu.

'The usual,' said Marshall, not taking the menu from her.

'I don't know what the usual is, sir, having been off for a week. But I know they've got some raspberries in, special.'

'Bring me what you like. What's your name?'

'Michelene.'

'Good lord.'

'*I'll* have some raspberries, Michelene,' said Sylvia, who these days could reasonably be called portly. 'And cream.'

'Very well, madam.'

She left with a glance at Marshall, which Sylvia considered forward. The sort of glance a nurse might direct at a patient when that nurse had been told things about that patient, thought Sylvia. She would describe it to Jack. Jack would make a lewd remark. She liked it when Jack made lewd remarks in private. He had once asked her to dress up in a nurse's uniform. She thought people only suggested things like that in trashy books and films. She had refused, but might agree if he asked her again. Nicely. But would he? He hadn't mentioned it for years.

'How did you know I was here? Clever of you, Sylvia. Or did you employ detectives?'

9

'I rang Jane. She was her usual unhelpful self. But I wheedled it out of her.'

'Nobody ever wheedled anything out of Jane.'

'She probably felt I ought to know what had become of you.'

4

Marshall's father was too young to fight in the first, too old to fight in the second war, but men who were not came to Tall Trees in uniform, and thrashed the rhododendrons with their swagger sticks. There was much extravagant saluting. Sir Jim, as Marshall's father was affectionately known, used to growl at these formal young men: 'Oh, don't be such blithering idiots, you're not on parade now,' but it pleased him none the less, and, if they called him sir deferentially and often, he would bring out the best port and waste it on them. Jane had just been promoted to house-keeper.

Marshall was his mother's favourite, Sylvia his father's. But when Marshall's mother died so young Marshall felt abandoned, became solitary, skulked in corners. Because of the bombing his boarding-school had been removed to the Yorkshire moors. The food was tasteless and inadequate and the teachers worse, a disreputable bunch, but it was better than the holidays. Sylvia, tiny then but with a defiantly cocked chin, was not sympathetic.

'You're always hanging about. Why don't you do something?'

'Like what?'

'Like a hobby. Train sets, or jigsaws, or stamp collecting, or something –'

'Train sets?' The idea was so absurd that both collapsed in giggles.

Sylvia was sent to the local school. When Marshall returned for the holidays he found the Grand Old Man of British diplomacy besotted with the little girl. What had been going on between them in his absence? They had private jokes and a private language. Sylvia was encouraged to dress up in her mother's clothes. Marshall found it insufferable and bullied her when he felt he had a chance of getting away with it. Sylvia did not seem to mind being bullied, but smiled at him even while the fists pounded home, which made him even angrier.

5

'You must want to borrow money.'

Even Marshall was surprised at the intensity of the blush which suffused Sylvia's cheeks and neck. She turned and looked out of the window at the cemetery of a church, where in the days before the National Health Service plague victims had been dumped in open graves.

'Come, come, Sylvia, there's nothing shameful about asking for a loan from big brother. Just as there's nothing shameful in turning you down.'

Sylvia returned to the bedside and picked at the broderie anglaise on the bedcover. Machine-made, but a clever machine.

'Jack thought I should come,' she muttered.

'Jack thought so, did he? And Jane told you where to find me. What a lot of scurrying around while I just lie here at three hundred a night. And how is Jack these days? Still carrying his troubles round his neck like a St Bernard with a brandy-keg? I tell you, Sylvia, you were the best bloody thing that ever happened to him, and he did fuck-all to deserve you before or since.'

Sylvia remembered moments of gentleness with Jack but could not speak of that to Marshall, of course. She was not a woman men found it easy to be gentle to, and such moments were sweeter than ever for their rarity. She remembered Jack; and another.

'Jack's fine,' she said. 'Your language hasn't improved.'

'Dying's like that. Has Jack still got a job?'

'Of course he has.'

'Many haven't. And Jack's scarcely an asset, I would have thought, to a company in recession.'

'It's his company. Well, I'm a director, so it's ours, I suppose.'

'How much money do you need?'

After Sylvia had named the figure, Marshall said: 'I assume you've doubled the amount you actually need, so I'll halve it,' and wrote her two cheques for a quarter of the amount requested, one with the current date, one with a date a month later. He was also concerned to cross each cheque and to make both out carefully in his sister's name.

'Tough on Jack,' he said as he folded them and handed them over. Sylvia responded with a February smile.

'You're a brick,' she said. 'Well, a half-brick.'

'Have your children visit me. I'll be suitably avuncular. Might even leave them something in my will.'

He had wanted her to go but was desolate when she had gone.

Although his symptoms were consistent with the diagnosis, it was hard to accept what the doctors had told him, since he felt no pain. He placed the fingers of his right hand round his heart and pressed, hard enough to leave etiolated prints on his skin. Nothing. Of course they had been feeding him their precious analgesic pills. But still why was there no pain?

For an undisturbed hour he took the best part of his grief out of its box with a pair of tweezers, and held it up to the light, searching for flaws.

It is unusual to find a stamp in perfect condition. Most collectors do not wish to. They hope for some insignificant inadequacy, one which in no way detracts from the appearance of the stamp but which enables them to renegotiate the price in their favour. The stamp should be well centred. It must not have been repaired or restored; if mint it must have its full complement of original gum. If used there is the important matter of its cancellation. This should be light, postal rather than 'cancelled-to-order', well placed and attractively clear. If it links the stamp to a 'piece', a 'front' or an 'entire', so much the better. Hinges or the remains of hinges are unwelcome. The perforations, if it is perforated, should be of equal length, and continue to the corners of the stamp. Its colour must not be faded, it must be free of rust marks, it must not be 'thinned', nor – and this was where the assessment became subjective – too perfect. With some stamps Marshall felt a buzz of alarm because they were precisely too good to be true. These were like copies of great pictures, crafted by skilled students, placed in antique frames and carefully varnished. One just knew. Marshall had once inquired of a member of the Royal Philatelic Society whether he too shared this recurrent unease when a rare but perfect stamp appeared at the committee of experts for validation. What did the committee report?

'What can we do?' the expert had replied. 'We have to give the validation of course. But five times out of ten we learn later of a clever faker at work, a new one to us, and in the other five cases there probably is one but he has yet to be unmasked. A high degree of perfection is always suspect. In collectors perhaps as well as in stamps. And yet we are there as a committee to demand perfection. It's onerous.'

So it was with Marshall's grief. Because it was new to him, this intimation of mortality, he could find no flaw in it. If the doctors were threatening him with dangerous surgery, or an amputation, or some reduction in his conditions of life – blindness, say, or impotence – the stamps would be flawed. But this grief, overwhelming in its finality, was too good to be true. Except in one particular. 'Perhaps weeks, possibly months, and it could even be years.' 'Could even' – that was hard to cope with. He wondered whether to canvass a second opinion and to demand details. A money-back guarantee. You must be more definite than that, he would say. Tell me six months, a year, or even two. Say: That's your limit. It may be anytime but that's your best shot.

He would get that Arab doctor back and put it to him: were you just having regard to my feelings? Because I would much prefer it if you didn't. What did you mean by 'could even'? I'm paying you three hundred a day. 'Could even' sounds like National Health treatment. You should be able to do better than that.

Marshall found that his grief could be subdivided. There was one album labelled 'Future Pain', one 'Loss of Ego', and one 'Unfinished Business'. There was a small stock book marked 'Absent Friends', and he opened that one first.

He was sixty. How many friends could one expect to acquire in sixty years? Whenever he read obituaries, or memoirs, or diaries, he was appalled at these promiscuous people who seemed to pick up friends at all stages of their lives, as though they were walking through bracken, burrs adhering to them as they passed by. But burrs could be shaken off. Friends less easily.

Had he wished for friends? Not really.

There were the women. He thought of them clothed, he thought of them naked, and then he clothed them again in his mind. How many of them would he really miss? Would any of them miss him? Jacqueline would have. He missed her, even now. Once, making love to her, he had understood what all the fuss was about and had murmured: 'This is the happiest moment of my life.' She had smiled and said: 'There will be others.' He must leave careful instructions that the funeral was to be strictly private. It could become a messy business if those other harpies arrived. He tried to imagine what Sylvia would think – how her initially charitable feelings would sour to disapproval and then, as the chapel of rest filled with his doxies, to outrage. Middle-aged mostly, he supposed, they would meet outside in the wintry sunshine (winter? Why did he imagine he would survive to see another winter? But clearly in his mind the scene was a winter scene with a crust of ice adrift on the larger puddles, and Sylvia's frosty words puffing out of her mouth, and the women replying in inimical smoke-screens). He saw Mandy from the office in one of those dreadful fur coats she affected – 'fun-furs' she called them, as though someone or something had gained any fun from them – and Hilary wearing a Burberry lined with tartan, and Jacqueline – now what would Jacqueline be wearing? – oh, of course, a shroud!

When he had first been aware of the pain around his heart – for there was pain before they brought him in here – he had regarded it as a personal outrage. How dared it? For several months he had dosed the pain with brandy, and for days at a time it had slumbered. Then it had clamped its jaws on him and refused to let go.

Future pain. Would it be painful? He hated the idea of pain. But it was hard to believe that in a hospital as grand as this one pain would be allowed past the security guards in the vestibule. Marshall was not a great hospital visitor. He preferred visiting prisons. Visiting a prison there was an unspoken assumption of superiority attaching to the visitor, and they rang a bell when you had had enough; in hospital the one who was free to come and go carried guilt not superiority about their person. But it had been his experience that hospital patients either felt little pain, or displayed none of what they felt. You saw men and women weeping in prison, not in hospital. Or else, when the pain became acute, the beds were screened and visitors kept away. We were protected from so much in life that was messy and uncontrollable. It was best for us to be kept in ignorance; air-conditioned, doubly glazed. He would tell the doctor that they were not to allow him to be in pain. That was their job, especially when he was paying. It was his job (or the PPP's) to reward them accordingly.

Loss of ego was the real killer. He had been at his mother's bedside when she died. He had yelled until they had permitted it; Jane was to tell him later that his mother had also requested it. He remembered her face now as it relaxed into death. One moment she was his beautiful mother in a silk peignoir; the next just a body. Within six weeks, six months, six years he would cease to be. This was a stamp awesome in its perfection. He would hold it up to the light many times in the coming weeks, front and back. Maybe he could find learned articles on it. Experts to validate it. But ultimately there was little to be done about it. Unlike Unfinished Business. Unfinished Business came under the heading of Portugal, the Faroe Islands and Mauritius. Unfinished Business required his immediate attention. He pressed the bell which lay so invitingly beside him. There was no time to lose. 'When I have fears that I may cease to be . . . ' What was that poem? How did it continue? 'When I have fears . . .' Young men in uniforms thrashing the rhododos with their swagger sticks . . . The Faroe Islands . . . Jacqueline . . . Was it Milton or Keats or Shakespeare? A poem a week they had had to learn. Every Sunday. How many could he still remember? When I have fears . . . Not even one. Sylvia, Jacqueline. His mother . . . Not one.

6

*M*arshall's career had been solid and unspectacular. He had chosen to read Politics, Philosophy and Economics at Oxford, and was able to take his place at New College with a closed scholarship from his public school. PPE – what a combination! Politics, the study of the art of the possible. Philosophy, the study of the art of the impossible. Economics, the study of the art of housekeeping. Three in one. The trinity that encompasses all things. What can be known, what can be done, what can be paid for. Everything else is dross. Not that it much mattered what you chose to read. As long as you could attend the lectures of Pevsner and Coghill, Tolkien and Berlin. Marshall, with the library at Tall Trees to snoop in, and his father's feet to sit at while absorbing scurrilous tales of the rich and famous, had a privileged position from which to hold forth on subjects fashionable at the time – the break-up of one empire, America's doomed attempt to hang on to another in south-east Asia, and the mercurial nature of the British Establishment.

So he acquired his First at the same time as he acquired his moustache, and with about as much effort, and then took a year at the Harvard Business School, where he wore button-down shirts and learnt about making money, and two years in a light infantry regiment where he learnt about sex and tribalism and survival (they called it basic training) and walking faster than other regiments, until with his commission he learnt about dignity, courtesy, poker, and when to drink claret and when burgundy. There was little that Marshall did not know *about* when he came home from Munchen-Gladbach, but really very little – when you compared him to his contemporaries – that he knew.

With a push and a shove from his father, Marshall was sent to a Civil Service weekend with words of encouragement buzzing in his brain. 'You'll be fine just so long as you don't blow your nose on the tablecloth.' Which he was, because he didn't. That was how, in his mid-twenties, with his moustache gone and his button-down shirts discarded, he found himself in the Treasury as what was called a development economist advising the Under-Secretary, who had the irritating habit of reading the prepared brief, listening politely to the justifying arguments, and snorting derisively.

The message had reached Marshall when he was attending an especially important conference in Stockholm in the late Sixties. He had delivered a paper the previous evening and was now basking in the approval of the other delegates. The paper was on The Financial Implications of Third World Aid, and argued with wit and lucidity the unfashionable view that the best thing the West could do for the Third World nations was to leave them well alone. If their assets and enterprise were valuable to the West, then multinational companies would beat at their door. They were best-placed to offer financial incentives; practical financial aid would bring political stability; the economic miracle which all affected to desire would follow as surely as riots followed independence.

Marshall called his paper 'Loaves and Fishes', and it began with a lengthy and hostile dissection of soft-bellied sentimentalism. A detailed parenthesis on Vietnam ('bad policy and worse public relations') followed. Then the peroration. 'Splendid –' said those delegates who had bothered to attend his lecture (a banquet had been laid on and a visit to the Royal Swedish Ballet and it was not easy to take in all three events) '– resolute in its mature perspicacity and good sense.' O'Malley was to deliver *his* paper on the evening of the day on which the telegram arrived, and Marshall intended to lead the attack on what was likely to be a paltry piece of work calling for altruistic self-abasement and a kind of Milly Molly Mandy attitude to world problems. At the welcoming reception O'Malley had been fool enough to leave his briefcase unattended and Marshall had grabbed the moment (which, after all, was just what the Sixties was about). A quick glance and the notes for O'Malley's address were located. As predicted, they contained disgracefully specious premises from which the rickety arguments depended, like doors rusting off their hinges. Apply a little sustained pressure and down they would tumble, O'Malley's inflated reputation with them. In the couple of intervening days Marshall had looked up some useful references and O'Malley was his for the taking. Then this telegram:

COME AT ONCE. YOUR FATHER CRITICAL. JANE.

Marshall could have pretended that the telegram had not reached him until after O'Malley's lecture. Then he could have made haste to arrive too late. But Manikum, the organising secretary who bustled around the delegates like an officious customs inspector, had asked for the telephone operator to read the telegram to him, Manikum, before visible confirmation was dispatched. Now the world and his wife knew and commiserated. Even O'Malley had the gall to approach him in the refectory and wheedle:

'So sorry about your father. Formidable man. Terrible time for you. So upsetting. And I had been so looking forward to hearing your reactions to my little paper. What a shame!'

On the other hand, Marshall speculated as he chewed his

way through the in-flight lunch (how did they manage to make caviare taste like pilchards?), it was just possible that he had been summoned for a last-gasp reconciliation.

My poor fellow, how I have misjudged you all these years! But at least God has granted me this final opportunity to make my peace with you. Give me your hand, me boyo. Let me enjoy for a few precious minutes the benison of your presence. Oh, and by the way the house, and everything in it, as well as my personal fortune, is yours, and Sylvia can whistle for it!

The fantasy was an endearing one, and a good deal pleasanter than the sprawling suburban blight that glowered at him from beyond the port-hole window. But it bore no relationship to any recognisable kind of reality. What for instance was this 'me boyo' stuff? His father was not Welsh. It was as though Marshall's imagination had realised the improbability of the scenario and had turned it into low farce. 'Your father critical'. Hadn't he always been?

Tall Trees was a large gloomy house a long way after Lutyens but with a few Gothic touches that attested more to the architect's limitations than to his learning. It was approached along an avenue of disheartening yews. By the time one reached the house one's spirits had been sufficiently lowered to expect the worst, expectations which the house confirmed. As he now approached it, Marshall observed with displeasure that dilapidation had set in. The creeper had got out of all control. The rhododendrons were paltry, the mulberry tree a stump, and the tennis court a garden centre for weeds. House martins were resting under the eaves. The paintwork had impetigo.

A cluster of doctors emerged from the house as he parked the car. There were contrived smiles on their hangdog faces. As to whether these smiles indicated a worsening or a recovery Marshall chose not to guess.

In the event and over some sweet sherry they gave him their prognosis. His father was still alive (all three consultants agreed on that) but sinking fast. He might survive the night; probably would. After that it was in the hands of God.

'God, gentlemen? I had no idea He formed a part of your prognosis.'

'A figure of speech merely.'

'So there *is* something you can do?' The doctors looked at him, then at each other.

He dismissed the medical men and told Jane, the house-keeper, to take the evening off. He would summon her, as she had him, if things became desperate. Jane, who had always had a soft spot for Marshall, simpered and left. Now Marshall was alone in the presence of the Great Man Himself.

Looking at the sleeping and emaciated face Marshall tried to recall him in full fig. That great chin thrust forward, those cornflower-blue eyes used to such great effect, whether to dazzle a supporter or to debilitate an opponent, those rolling tones, a consequence some said of his Welsh upbringing, although the Great Man Himself had never lived in Wales, had only visited Wales when necessity or ambition dictated such a visit. Good to be thought Welsh, was the Great Man Himself's view, because class counts for less, and is less easily delineated, with a regional accent. So without affecting to be Welsh, he never disabused those who assumed Welshness in him, and when he became known by journalists as the Dragon, he let that stand too, arguing – or being prepared to argue – that there had been dragons in England, and what about St George? A reporter would have to be both perspicacious and pedantic to point out that to the Welsh a dragon was heroic, to the English a princess-roaster.

Oh those blue eyes, what couldn't the man do with them!

'Better than policies,' remarked his agent.

And the ploys he perfected in his political career he practised on his family. He opened his blue eyes suddenly and focused them on Marshall.

'You here?'

'Yes, Dad.'

'What for?'

'I was sent for by Jane.'

'Ridiculous. What does a housekeeper know? Just a bout of indigestion. Bloody doctors can't agree, of course. One says one thing, one says another. What the poor patient's supposed to think, heaven only knows. Not supposed to think, I suppose. What did they tell you?'

'You want the truth?'

'Of course I bloody do. Why shouldn't I?'

'Because it's not good. They say it's serious, Dad.'

Seeing his father in his navy silk pyjamas, jaunty once, monogrammed in pink over the breast pocket, Marshall felt that he would miss the Great Mad Hypocrite, that he would remember his virtues more vividly than his shortcomings, that he might grow to love the memory of a dead monster, so much easier to love than a living one.

Something had gone wrong with his father's political career in the Fifties. One moment he had been making policy, the next pontificating upon it. Churchill had depended upon him, ringing him at all hours of the day and, especially, night, summoning him into bedroom, bathroom or summerhouse for 'serious talks' about Eisenhower, about literature, about Rothschild, about art. With Churchill's decline into senility, Sir Jim had no longer been much in demand at Central Office. Nobody thanked you for advising against Suez, or taking a tough line with Khrushchev. Not that he had always been right. He had often spoken out in favour of housing the homeless and funding the arts. Heretical stuff!

But he did not plummet so much as gently spiral like a falling leaf into desuetude. The BBC loved him, those gravelly tones, that irreverence, those intimate recollections of the Great and the Good. They grovelled to him. Until one day the grovelling stopped, along with the invitations to pontificate. A new and meticulous Director-General had heard and believed some gossip, and had issued an edict; anyway younger and more radical colleagues were in vogue. Sir Jim was hurt, he was puzzled, he was furious. He became a hermit in his hideous house, raving at the young. He wrote to the newspapers, bludgeoning, intemperate letters on eccentric topics. His blue eyes blazed, his throat rasped, these were the death throes of a species becoming extinct. Marshall's heart had bled for him then, as it did for him now. Until the old man said:

'I've left everything to Sylvia. I had Thingy Whatsit round to tie up the details. In case the doctors are right, which, I suppose, is possible.'

'I don't believe you.'

'No reason why you should. Doesn't matter really, does it?'

'But *why*, Dad?'

'Whim. Plus a feeling in my gut that you'll be all right – you are already – and Sylvia might not.'

'This is outrageous.'

His dying father turned his baby blue eyes on Marshall. 'I know. But you'll just have to get used to it. Besides, you understand all about money. You always boast about your investments. You can make as much as you like if you set your mind to it.'

'Sylvia can too. She's got an excellent job.'

'Women's work. Not that there's that much. I'm sorry, old lad. Wrong-headed of me, I expect, but I'm too tired to go through it all again. Made a lot of mistakes in my life, so this is par for the course, eh?' And almost instantaneously he was asleep, his mouth open, exposing missing teeth, his breath rasping. But then he opened his eyes again surprisingly and muttered:

'I'm going to sleep now. Thought I'd just mention this pecuniary matter in case you felt like putting a pillow over my face. Wouldn't like to go like that, you see. Let my body decide. Far better, don't you agree?' And then with irresistible

25

charm: 'Myself, I blame the unions!'

When his father was well asleep, Marshall crept from the master bedroom, which smelt of air freshener, not as the label promised, of the Dewy Pungency of a Woodland Glade, but of some sickly-sour concoction of a perfume panel's deliberations.

So Sylvia would get the lot. Well, she had always been the favourite. Marshall recalled seeing her and the old man huddled over the crossword, chortling over the complications of some arcane clue. At such times they looked less like father and daughter than siblings, both with the light brown hair, the savagely blue eyes, the long patrician nose and the smooth skin of the well-fed and the well-protected. He, Marshall, had taken after his mother. His features were small and regular, his face round, not oval, his eyes brown, his hair dark. She might have inherited the money, but not the prettiness. Marshall could make no sense of the crossword, but turned instead to the arts columns, and read the critics with a rare passion. Father critical. In later life, Marshall would attend concerts regularly twice or thrice a week and write furious letters to those critics who seemed to him most blinkered or most malicious. When one of them wrote that where Chopin was concerned Iturbi could not hold a candle to Rubinstein, Marshall turned up at the journalist's house and refused to leave until the journalist agreed to listen to a polonaise recorded by both pianists. The critic stuck to his guns, of course, but Marshall fancied that thereafter his column was a touch more circumspect, and even at times apologetic. So Sylvia was to get the lot.

It was wholly unjust. Marshall roamed the house making a mental inventory of everything which would be Sylvia's, from the Augustus Johns in the sitting room, effete scribbly things but valuable, to the jade in the display case in the study. Did his father mean her to have *everything*? There was nothing vague about what he had said. Everything? It was a ruthless word to use. Perhaps Marshall would have a legal claim to a fair division of the spoils. He would have to consult Battersby in the morning. But if the will turned out to be as uncompromising as the old man had hinted, Marshall could not imagine a court overturning it.

As he toured the house, his outrage simmered and thickened. By the time he reached the attic, he was shaking and muttering with the injustice of it all. Battersby was a competent lawyer. He paid Battersby generously. Battersby would have to find a loophole.

The attic was awash with the grey light of incipient dawn. Marshall had not climbed the stepladder to this gloomy place since he was a boy. Spread out in front of him and piled high were dozens, scores, hundreds, maybe, of cartons. Why hadn't the weight of them brought down the ceilings? What on earth were they? Where had they come from? How long had they been there? By the light of a heavy-duty torch he examined the contents first of one, then a second, then a third.

The dawn chorus was raucous by the time he stretched his length on the bed he had slept in as a child; too short for him now by at least a foot. Marshall found comfort in the buttercup pattern on the eiderdown, in the drawer full of adolescent love letters, written but not sent, received but not replied to, and reciprocated with a snapshot attached. He lay in some discomfort and heard the mice scurrying around the wainscot, the death-watch beetle in the rafters, the house martins restless under the eaves. He resolved upon a plan.

7

Marshall woke up to a new day with the expectation that he might not see the end of it. Each morning he hoped that his illness was a dream, until the discomfort persuaded him otherwise. There was a nurse on duty whom he did not recognise and it seemed that either she did not know or chose to ignore the gravity of his condition. She was young and cheerful and told him, in response to his query, that she was from County Clare, and that her name was Stacey Anne.

'Sure, Lahinch is not much of a town, sir, but we have two fine international golf courses, and a restaurant where you can spend twenty punts on your dinner, sir, and not notice the change. You should come and visit us there, sir, for the sea air would do you the world of good. You could come in August and enjoy the festival of the Darlin' Girls from Clare. That's quite an event sir, and indeed did I not enter it myself when I was a young sprig of a thing? Last year, to be sure.'

'Did you win the competition, Stacey Anne?'

'Indeed no, sir, I did not, Fidelina Mulkere won it, and didn't she go off with one of the judges back to Limerick? For the shopping, she said.'

'That was remiss of her.'

'And of him, to my way of thinking. Shopping's one word for it. Now would you credit the cheek of the girl? Shall I tell you the prizes she won, quite apart from the prize her fancy man left her with, which I fancy she could well have done without?'

'What were her prizes?'

'Well let me see now. There was a thousand punts in cash, sir, and a crystal trophy, and two Aer Lingus tickets to New York, and a year's free hairstyling, and a perpetual silver salver, and a weekend for two in Mullingar, and a Cognito outfit from that nice boutique in Ennis, sir, and some hand-crafted jewellery, and tours and receptions and such a grand round of festivities as I could not even describe, sir. But for myself, I would have wanted nothing more than the perpetual silver salver engraved with my name as the Darlin' Girl, and passed on all the rest. I liked the idea of something perpetual, sir, and I still do. Sure, it's nice to be remembered, whether as a Darlin' Girl or anything else, come to that. Would you take breakfast now, sir? I could find you a pair of kippers if you felt so inclined. Take the bones out, sir, if you like, as I do for some of the other gentlemen.'

Later in the morning of the day on which he feared he might die, Marshall received a visit from Jane, his father's house-keeper and latterly his own.

'You asked me to bring you your mail, sir, although I am not to cause you any anxiety so I was unsure whether you would be made more anxious by my bringing it or by my not bringing it.'

'You did right to bring it, Jane, for after all I am the one who employs you, just as I employ this clinic to kill me slowly.'

'Oh, sir, surely not. While there's life there's hope.'

There were tears swelling in the good but tiresome woman's eyes. She removed her spectacles the better to wipe the tears away.

'While there's life, Jane, there's incompetence and a lot of fuss, that's exactly what there is. And some pain too which I could well do without.'

'I have taken the telephone off the hook, sir, because news of your indisposition has leaked out, and they keep ringing to inquire, even a newspaper, sir, but not one of our newspapers –'

'That was a sensible thing to do, Jane. However –'

'However, sir, your fact machine could not be taken off its hook, and I dared not interfere with it lest I do it some mischief, and that has been sending me messages and demanding answers from me which I cannot give, sir, not understanding how the thing works!' At which she removed from a Sainsbury's carrier bag a long and ill-organised roll of fax paper.

'I'll look at it later, Jane, because just now I feel overcome with tiredness. Leave me the letters too, and when you next come and see me I'll tell you whether anything requires any answer.'

Marshall had used tiredness as his excuse but no sooner had he uttered the word than he felt an exhaustion of body and spirit. Within a couple of minutes, he was asleep and wheezing through his open mouth.

8

Sylvia arrived at Tall Trees at nine and Marshall was still asleep. He had slept for a few hours in his boyish bed with a sleep of boyish sweetness. Sylvia was not blessed with the gift of quietude, and the squealing of brakes, the shouting of instructions, the crunch of gravel and the banging of doors were loud and prolonged. There was nobody could punish a car's door the way Sylvia could.

Marshall was confused. Where was he or, even more to the point, who was he? The wallpaper and the old-fashioned furniture made him believe that he was a child again. It was depressing when the frailties of his thickening body reminded him of how little he still belonged in this room, and it was with a lowering of the spirits that he recalled why he was in this house. As he sat up in bed in a room that seemed to have shrunk around him, and listened to Sylvia's disturbances, he remembered what his father had told him of his intentions towards Sylvia and himself. And as he sprinkled expensive after-shave on his cheeks he remembered the cartons in the loft.

Jane knocked on his door. 'I thought it best to tell you, sir, that Miss Sylvia has arrived and that your father passed a peaceful night and that the doctors will be returning soon. It is nice seeing you in this old bed. You are still the tidiest sleeper I ever did see.'

'Has my sister breakfasted?'

'She is doing so now, sir. Would you care to join her? There's plenty of fresh coffee in the pot.'

Marshall was amused at the contrast between Sylvia's first words and the determined way in which she was packing away her scrambled eggs.

'Jane tells me Dad's dying.'

'Everybody seems to agree on that, except the man himself. Have you seen him, Sylvia?'

'I looked in on him. He was fast asleep though. Sleeping the sleep of the just.'

'If you believe that . . . ' said Marshall, pouring coffee.

'He was no worse than many, and better than some,' said Sylvia, taking his part with traditional lack of scruple. 'And why am I using the past tense? He's not a man to do what doctors – or anyone else – tells him to do. Remember how he stood up to Beaverbrook over that rearmaments business?'

'Well, Sylvia, your loyalty to him has been rewarded.'

'I don't understand you. And even if you mean what I think you mean, this is scarcely the moment to discuss it.'

'Why not? When better?'

'Because I've travelled all night to be here, Marshall. I was with an important client in Boston when I got Jane's telegram, and it was by no means a straightforward matter to drop everything and come here directly.'

'Are you upset that you've come too soon? Are you so apprehensive that you'll lose your important client?'

Sylvia thought of a patio overlooking a grassy valley, of long drinks in frosted glasses, of the benevolent lined face of the company lawyer, and the expensive clothes of his wife, family and entourage. Then she looked at her brother with affectionate disapproval.

'You have a way of putting things, Marshall, as though you would welcome a confrontation. We're not as close as we should be, but we're not enemies, are we?'

Marshall agreed that they were not, and then, encouraged by a mouthful of strong coffee, said: 'He tells me he's left everything to you. Can your important client in Boston match that?'

Marshall watched her closely as he spoke. She looked tired but strong. She must have taken expensive advice on how to make the best of herself. Her blond hair no longer straggled, but had been cut short so that a lock falling to one side added a feminine and charming touch to a sensible style. From whom had she been taking advice? Not Jack. He would have had her in tartan hot-pants and a see-through blouse. But this outfit was Chanel, or the next best thing. Marshall remembered that, as a girl, Sylvia had found it difficult to attract men, but had attracted the pretty girls who wished to discuss men with her. More than once Marshall had benefited from Sylvia's confidantes, and Sylvia had permitted him to, perhaps feeling that a few weeks' attention from her big brother would be a helpful antidote to an altogether unsuitable lover. As good as, and cheaper than, a holiday in the sun.

'You know what Dad's like. He's quite capable of telling you something, simply in order to gauge your reaction. I think you shouldn't jump to conclusions.'

'He gave me his reasons. He said that you'd make a better go of it, whatever that means.'

Sylvia forked the last of her scrambled eggs into her mouth and stood up:

'I still don't want to discuss this now, Marshall. I want to see him before the doctors arrive and mess him about.'

'Do you want to see him alone?'

'Would you mind?'

'Of course not. It's all yours. Literally.'

As she passed his chair she put a hand briefly on the back of his neck. It seemed halfway between the caress of a lover and the blade of a guillotine. Within a couple of minutes she was back, fumbling with the door-handle, stumbling into the room, her face drenched with tears.

'Dad's dead, Marshall, he's dead.'

9

Marshall awoke feeling refreshed. He had been dreaming of the seaside resort in Brittany he had visited with Sylvia and his father some forty-five years ago. There was a sandy path through pine trees, which led to a golden beach. As you reached the end of the forest, it was like a door opening on the Atlantic. There was sun and a fresh breeze, and the mingled scents of salt and ozone, seaweed and pine. In his dream the sun had been warm on his cheeks, the breakers had been roaring in, and there were donkeys to ride, and vanilla ice cream between wafers.

While he slept they had tidied his room. There was a vase of spring flowers on the bedside table, and the double windows had been flung wide. The pile of letters and the roll of fax paper awaited him. There was a letter postmarked Carcassonne and addressed in a meticulous hand. The letter had been stamped with one of the handsome French series of art reproductions. It was better than a signature. His impatience to read what Marcel had to say conflicted with a philatelist's abomination of mutilating the envelope. He had no paper-knife to hand so he sliced it open carefully with a pair of nail scissors.

My dear Marshall,

Your troubles are at an end. At least as far as Portugal is

concerned, my friend. I have the 1853 set, precisely as you would desire it, in the original and in the cancelled form, with the shade varieties and all perforations intact. I have too the double impression of the fifty-reis. Even you, with your inviolate standards, will be unable to find fault with these beautiful examples. The price, as always, is astonishingly reasonable, given the rarity of this set. I speak of F300,000. For you, dear Marshall, I turn myself into a charity, it seems.

I await from you an early response. I need not stress that I have other clients, and notably that crook Yegerova, willing to pay me double the modest reimbursement I require from you, my old comrade. But loyalty to a friend has always seemed more important to me than profit. As you well know.

So send to me your instructions, or come yourself. If you can make it to Carcassonne I look forward to sharing a bottle of Montrachet and a canard en casserole at Chez Victor. I would willingly have come to you, my friend, but that there are outstanding formalities relating to my passport, which make it inconvenient to travel just now. I would also take pleasure in delighting your eyes with a recent acquisition, some proud beauties from the Côte d'Ivoire.

But that suffices, my friend, for the moment. I remain, in anticipation of a happy outcome,

Assuredly your old comrade,
Marcel

Could it be true? The Portugal set? With the shade varieties? Difficult stamps, all of them. If it had been any one of a number of other dealers, Nevinsky, for instance, or Thirkell, or the dubious Castleton, Marshall would have sighed and prepared himself for a predictable disappointment. They were not all crooked, these fellows, some were merely ignorant, although that had worked in Marshall's favour in the past. That idiot, Andersson, seemed able to acquire excellent stock from sources unavailable to the rest of the trade (everyone suspected nefarious practices but nothing had ever been – nothing would ever be – proved). However Andersson never knew just what he had acquired. Once he had shown Marshall a stock book filled with Heligoland, and laughed at such unconvincing reprints. Marshall had laughed with him and purchased the collection for a derisory sum 'because after all every collector should keep a number of forgeries and reprints as an awful warning'. Marshall had continued chuckling all the way home in the taxi, as he salivated over the splendid selection, several on fronts and one or two on entires linked by delightful cancellations from the Centre for Marine Biology.

Marcel was one of the old school. His expertise was limited to European countries, but what he did not know about those was scarcely worth the knowing. Indeed a validation by Marcel was worth far more than one by any of the philatelic associations. Reading the letter Marshall was aware of a familiar and welcome response: a quickening of the pulse, a dryness in the mouth, and a greed for ownership that could not be denied. But almost at once an overwhelming and deplorable pain seemed to spread from his centre, like the bud of a huge flower swelling and bursting inside him. There was beauty in the pain too. When it seemed as if the flower could expand no further, Marshall lost consciousness.

10

*T*he doctors and the undertakers were quickly disposed of, as was the body, still weighty despite months of emaciation, of the Great Man Himself. Only Sylvia, Marshall and Jane remained in the hulk of the huge house.

Jane was in despair. She sat down and stood up and sat down again. She took some darning out of a tapestry bag with wooden handles, then replaced it. She announced that she would make them all a cup of tea, then returned from the kitchen with no memory of what she intended to do there.

'Do sit down and be quiet, Jane,' Sylvia snapped. 'It does no one any good to flap around like that.'

'She's right, Jane. You must pull yourself together.'

'But no one will have me. I shall be a useless old person.'

Sylvia glared at the housekeeper. 'If you carry on like that I'm quite sure no one will have you, Jane. And as to being useless, you offered to make us both a cup of tea and where is it? Useless is as useless does. Or doesn't do. Mr Marshall and I have things to discuss, the breakfast has not been washed up, and a cup of tea would be extremely welcome.'

Sylvia's stern tones succeeded where Marshall's sympathy had not. Jane left.

'Conditioning,' said Sylvia. 'There's a woman who for more than thirty years has done exactly as she's told, and the consequence is, she's quite incapable of independent action. It's a paradigm of the history of the British working class. We would actually be doing her a kindness if we let her go without a penny to her name. Domestic Thatcherism. Could be the making of her.'

'But Sylvia, she's too old for that, and too tired. And maybe it's not just conditioning, maybe it's the way she is.'

Sylvia and Marshall were sitting at either end of the sofa. Neither had cared to take up residence in the armchair which was their father's by custom and practice. There were patches on the arms where his hands had rested, and a faded antimacassar. Marshall thought it unnatural to be looking at his sister in profile.

Sylvia asked: 'You didn't want to see him before they took him away?'

'I saw him last night. He was very grumpy. I'd rather remember him grumpy than dead.'

Sylvia was thinking about Boston and the view over the grassy valley and the long drinks, and the money. Marshall was thinking about the money. Marshall said:

'I expect he lodged the will at Coutts, or with Winepress, or a copy with both. Should we ring Winepress up and alert him?'

'I've already done so,' said Sylvia. She glanced at his startled profile and caught him glancing at hers. 'I telephoned while the undertakers were doing their business. He's on the M4 as we speak.'

'If the will says what Father told me it said, can I make a suggestion?'

Sylvia smiled slightly. 'Suggest away.'

'If you get all the money and the house and the contents of the house, can I clear the attic?'

'You, Marshall, as a house-clearer? Hardly my perception of you. What would your colleagues in Stockholm have thought?'

'I'm not sure that wealth will become you, Sylvia. Sneering certainly doesn't. You used not to sneer.'

Sylvia moved closer to him, and surprised and rather alarmed Marshall by taking his hand. Hers was warm and soft and pleasantly pliant.

'I'm sorry. Of course you can take what you want. God alone knows what's up there. You'd actually take a load off my mind if you would clear it all away. But we had better wait and see what Winepress has to tell us.'

Arthur Winepress had the florid complexion that his name led you to expect. Sylvia seemed on surprisingly good terms with him, which took Marshall aback. Maybe Marshall should have arranged for Battersby to be there too. Winepress arrived in a shabby car, and left a boisterous retriever in it. He was courtesy itself when it came to the commiserations. He sounded sincere, kept them brief, and performed the role of family solicitor as if he had spent a month watching reruns of English films of the Forties and Fifties. He carried a Gladstone bag instead of a briefcase and changed his spectacles to read the will.

'Couldn't be more straightforward. Drew it up meself not long ago. No relatives, besides the two of you. He leaves the house, the contents and his investments, a list of which I have already obtained from his brokers, to Miss Marshall. He explains the reasons for his partiality in the will, and you must make of them what you must. Oh, there is the small matter of a bequest of ten pounds for each year she has spent in his service for Jane Hancock, the housekeeper. The investments amount to a little short of a hundred thousand pounds. After the statutory tax-free distributions, which will come from the value of the estate, there will be death duties upon the remainder.' The solicitor beamed equally upon the two of them. No partiality in his performance! 'It's a dangerous assumption, but in a case as straightforward as this, I cannot imagine that the granting of probate will take too long.

Obviously if I can serve you in any other capacity . . . '

Had Jane been listening at the door? The timing of her entrance with tea and egg-and-cress sandwiches seemed to suggest as much. Marshall observed her carefully, but was unable to decide whether she would be more likely to be insulted by the old man's meanness, or gratified by being remembered at all. Her demeanour gave nothing away.

As Sylvia was leaving, Marshall said:

'Just one thing, Sylvia. Dad left everything to you because he believed you'd make a better go of it than I would, whatever that means. If you don't, you've let us both down.'

At the time Marshall had no reason to suppose that she would, was indeed almost persuaded that his father had shown discernment in the ruthlessness of the will. Sylvia was clearly sure that he had. But all three of them were wrong.

11

In the deep well of his unconsciousness, there was hardly a glint of light. He was flying, floating, sinking. There was no bottom to this descent, but if the light was extinguished, he would fall or float or fly no longer.

Marshall was a heartbeat away from death.

His weariness, his cancer, the turgid coursing of his blood dragged him down and away from the light, but stronger than these was the sense of unfinished business.

Pictures were illuminated before him, they were lit, as if from within. He was in an exhibition, walking on soft carpets, in pitch darkness, but around him were these tiny glass cases. In one, a mass of highly coloured kings and queens and emperors, Manuel of Portugal, Louis of France, Hussein of Jordan, Haile Selassie of Ethiopia. In another, revolutionaries, Lenin and Bolívar, Castro and Garibaldi. In a third, explorers, Van Diemen and Magellan, Da Gama and Blériot. In a fourth, sportsmen. In a fifth, travellers in space. In a sixth, wildlife, the Canadian beaver, the kookaburra, the leopard, the kangaroo. In a seventh, Victoria full-face and profile, black and blue and red, young with a string of pearls, older with a bun, aged with a veil over her head. In an eighth, the other English monarchs. In a ninth, symbolic figures, the Curly Head, the Baby Face, Liberté, the Embossed Crown, the

Posthorn with Thunderbolts, the Maltese Cross, the Double-Headed Eagle, Hermes, Helvetia. In a tenth, butterflies, insects and fish. In an eleventh, trains and boats and cars and planes. And in a final cabinet, three display stands contained nothing; a clear light, a mounted sheet, something missing.

It was difficult to struggle back. It was fighting against gravity; worse, it was fighting against mortality. His lungs were bursting. The light flickered and seemed on the point of expiration. There was a soughing of a breeze which carried frost on its breath. But the light did not expire. He would not permit it. He had to clamber up the sides of the well, and it took all his strength.

The rungs of the ladder were rusted, and in some cases missing. More than once he lost his footing entirely, and dangled in space, his fingers tightening around the corroded metal bars, the pain in his arms and shoulders almost unendurable. But the frost had gone from the air. The light was brighter than it had been. He knew that this time he would reach it.

Stacey Anne was at his bedside when he came round. Marshall was aware of something cold at his wrist. He moved his head but could make out nothing more than cold shapes and patterns. He shivered. The dankness of the well was still around him.

'Back in the land of the living, eh? Sure we almost lost you there, sir.'

'I'm cold,' said Marshall.

'It's a cold day, for sure, sir.'

'What's that?' Marshall attempted to indicate by his head the novelty by his left hand.

'That's the old drip. We fatten you up for Christmas.'

She lowered her voice. 'Or Ramadan, in a place like this.'

'I know what a drip is,' muttered Marshall. 'And I know what it portends.'

'Ah, you may not be dying, Mr Marshall. There's some a

lot worse than you come back fit and rarin' to go. Have to tie 'em to their beds, some of them, after Dr Zilkha's had a go at them.'

Marshall considered this, but found concentration a problem. He asked Stacey Anne to come back later; he wanted to have a private confabulation with her. She was unsure what a confabulation was, but doubted whether it could be anything dirty, with the poor old creature dying like he was. But before the confabulation with Stacey Anne, Marshall received a private visit from Jack, who was staggering under the weight of a large bouquet of flowers, chrysanthemums predominating.

'I was halfway along the corridor when I thought: Bloody hell, will he take these the wrong way? I was going to bring chocolate fondants but your sister said you probably wouldn't be allowed them, so I switched horses in mid-stream.'

Jack and the horses, thought Marshall. Poor old Sylvia.

Jack was a large bluff man, who wore blazers, cravats and two-tone shoes. The last man alive to wear a cravat, thought Marshall. Jack's hair shone with grease, his trousers with sitting, his face with gratitude. He sat down heavily and placed the bouquet on the bed. A spray of foul-smelling water spattered Marshall's face.

'Came to thank you, old man. I sometimes think, it's a rotten old world, but then an act of generosity like yours, well it restores one's faith. Sylvia told me how you persuaded her to take the money, and I just wanted you to know how much we appreciated it. How're you feeling anyway? Your colour's good.'

Marshall's colour was not good. The whites of his eyes were yellowed like parchment, and his cheeks were flushed.

Marshall said drily: 'I'm doing all right. The nurse here told me that she'd seen worse than me get better.'

'Worse than you? She was joshing you, I'm sure.'

'Maybe.'

44

'Do you want to know what we'll do with the money?'

'Pay off your debts, I was given to understand. Then small luxuries like bread and milk. Clothes for the kids. That sort of thing.'

Jack leant forward, bright-eyed and as keen as if he were just starting out in life.

'We'll pay off the most pressing debts, of course. Most of them. But there's this brilliant scheme . . .'

The scheme, as outlined by Jack, was not just brilliant, but cast-iron. Jack's schemes usually were. He proposed a central kitchen in the West End of London, with a team of tireless haute-cuisine cooks. Restaurants which subscribed to the system could dispense with their own kitchens entirely. Just a fridge for the cold items, reordered daily, and a microwave for the hot ones. The punters choose from the menu – also supplied centrally if required – a fax is sent, an outrider is dispatched, and within ten minutes the mouth-watering selection is delivered to the back door, ready for garnishing and seasoning.

'I reckon that this scheme can reduce a restaurant's over-heads by at least seventy-five per cent – no need to shop in the markets, no wastage, a minimum of staff – and improve its profit margins out of all recognition. While at our end of the operation, catering in bulk, I don't see how we can go wrong.'

As Jack went on to describe the subtle and sophisticated dishes that his company – Cuisine Anonyme, he thought to call it – could concoct, Marshall's attention wandered. It seemed clumsy of Jack to talk of recipes to a man on a drip, Marshall thought. Could not be permitted. He realised that Jack had come to the end of his presentation when he heard him asking:

'So what do you think of that, eh?'

Marshall's view of Jack was blocked by several large and discouraging blooms.

'What will Sylvia's role be?'

'Our accountant and business adviser, of course. You know how good she is at that sort of thing.'

'What about your present job?'

'Ah.'

'Sylvia said –'

'Yes, well I'm not sure she was in full possession of the facts. Burdett and Gould, the company I work for, has ceased trading.'

'Are you not entitled to redundancy money?'

'There is none.'

'But you should have some sort of claim –'

'Let's just leave it that I haven't.' Jack's enthusiasm for changing the subject was blatant. 'And anyway new beginnings are what I came to talk to you about. Which is good news for you too. Because it means of course that we'll be able to pay back, with interest, your original investment.'

Exhausted by Jack's keenness, Marshall closed his eyes. 'I thought I was just being generous. If I had realised it was an investment,' he said, 'I would have avoided it like the plague. And get those sodding blooms off my bed.'

12

As soon as he was alone in Tall Trees, Marshall
returned to the attic, and carried the first carton down the
ladder to the landing, and thence to the drawing room. It was
weighty. The items it contained were wrapped in yellowing
newsprint, English, German, French and even what appeared
to be Hebrew. Marshall unwrapped the first parcel with
trembling fingers. It contained a lead soldier in the uniform of
the Duke of Wellington's Light Infantry. He marched proudly
forward, gun at the slope. Other soldiers followed, some
marching, some prone, guns at the ready, guns at the slope. A
troop of cavalry followed the infantry. Then some heavy
artillery. Every piece was perfect. At the bottom of the carton
two regiments, one of foot, one of horse, each in their original
Britain's boxes. Even without the boxed sets, Marshall
counted several hundred figures, more perhaps than the actual
survivors of the campaigns, and where those were stooped
and stumbling, these stood as proud and erect as any young
man who has been told (and believes) that it is up to him to
defend the honour of Queen and country. A tune came into
Marshall's head and he hummed it to himself.

'We're the soldiers of the Queen, my lads . . .
Who've seen, my lads,

Who've been, my lads,
In the fight for England's glory, lads
Of her worldwide glory let us sing . . . '

Marshall was of a generation which had not had wars to fight. They had passed him by. Others had fought. In Korea and in Vietnam, in Suez and in Israel, in Hungary and the Falklands, wars one read about, wars one watched with the after-dinner mints, war fought by regulars and mercenaries and UN troops, not by enlisted men. A nostalgia had grown up in Marshall and his contemporaries for the extremes of life; they felt they had missed out. The intensity of pain, and fear, the absolute dependence on friends, the necessity for unquestioning discipline, the frustrations of incompetent commanders, the rewards of unsullied sleep. Some spent long weekends in Hampshire and Surrey, spraying each other with scatterguns.

Marshall's generation turned instead to fighting for ownership, and status, the faster car, the sharper suit. One gave one's loyalty to one's oil company, one's friendship to one's line director.

'And when we say we've always won,
And when they ask us how it's done,
We'll proudly point to every one
Of England's soldiers of the Queen.'

Marshall replaced the soldiers in the carton. They would raise quite a sum if properly marketed. He wondered about the other cartons. He looked through a telephone directory and contacted a local carter. Move fast before Sylvia changed her mind.

Within hours the attic was empty and Marshall's spacious London flat so packed with cartons that he had difficulty picking his way to the lavatory.

His hands were shaking. He cancelled two appointments which his personal assistant had made for the following day. He unplugged the phone. He laid a sheet on the carpet. Then he began.

13

'*I*t's good of you to come, Stacey Anne. I hoped I could count on you. But I am quite without resources, stuck in this bed with this God-damn needle up my arm.'

'No need at all to upset yourself, Mr Marshall. I have come to settle you for the night, just that.'

'I am scared, Stacey Anne.'

'There will be somebody with you throughout the night. Me, I used to be scared of the dark too, so my mammy gave me a night-light. And wasn't I then scared of the shadows it cast?'

'Do they pay you well in this place?'

'Not so bad, Mr Marshall. But we have to find for our laundry and dry cleaning. And no perks.'

'I am considering employing you.'

'Are you indeed?'

'A delicate mission.'

'Would that make me a missionary?'

'I'll pay you double what they pay you here.'

'Sure, nothing is for nothing in this wicked world,' and Stacey Anne paused in her bedside ministrations. 'I learnt that with me mammy's milk, the only thing in life that *is* free. But there are some things a Darlin' Girl from Clare won't do, and that's the truth of it.' She added as an afterthought: 'But not too many. Do you want me to give you a bit of a show?'

'No,' said Marshall sadly. 'Another time, another place perhaps.'

Stacey Anne sat on the bed and eyed her patient with amused unconcern. 'So what *do* you want, O Master?'

'First of all – and you can do this in your lunch-hour – I want you to go to W. H. Smith and buy me two of these.'

He slipped a newspaper cutting from under his pillow, and passed it to her with his free hand. 'They will cost you about eighty pounds each, but Jane will give you the money if you ask her nicely.'

'Do I get to keep them afterwards – well, after whatever it is you're going to ask me to do?'

'One of them,' said Marshall. 'Regard it as a perk.'

The following afternoon Stacey Anne arrived back at Marshall's bedside with a small gaudily wrapped parcel. 'They said a free gift-wrapping with all goods costing over fifty quid, so I thought, Why not?'

'Open it.'

Within the wrapping were two boxes and the boxes opened to reveal two miniature tape recorders.

'I know what they are because it says on the box,' said Stacey Anne, 'but how do they work?'

'Well, we'll practise, shall we, till we're perfect?'

'If I were perfect,' said Stacey Anne tartly, 'I wouldn't be taking money or gifts from strange gentlemen.'

'Perfection is what it's all about,' said Marshall.

Then Marshall told her about Marcel and showed her the letter. She said she didn't understand. He said it was simple enough. He gave her the money, she went to Carcassonne, she gave Marcel the money and she returned with the stamps.

'What I don't understand,' said Stacey Anne, 'at all, is why you don't send him the money and have him send you the stamps.'

'It's an awful lot of money, my dear, and I have more

confidence in you than in the post offices of Britain and France. They are vandals.'

'But how can you be sure, sir, that I won't just take the money and run? There are plenty of girls, no question, who would do such a thing, Fidelina Mulkere for one.'

'Of course I thought of that. But if you intended to betray me, would you have asked that question?'

'I do not, sir, and no, I would not. But how will I know if the stamps are the right ones?'

'Marcel knows about these things and he knows that I know. My custom is more important to him than the short-term advantage of a quick and profitable deception. All serious collectors depend upon trustworthy dealers. I, now, more than most. And I want you to record the transaction on that machine. And Marcel to give me the technical details.'

Stacey Anne reoccupied her position on the bed and looked into Marshall's eyes.

'Does it matter so much to you?'

'Very much, Stacey Anne.'

'Ah well, in that case . . .'

14

*I*t took Marshall several years to work his way through the cartons. He drew up rules, the most important of which was never to open a new carton until he had worked his way through the previous one. Working his way was a complete process. Take the lead soldiers. Having unpacked them, he bought himself a book on the subject; also a price guide. Then he sold them.

He considered making contact with a mainstream collector, or setting up a market stall, or selling the army at auction. He concluded in the first case that a collector would be more knowledgeable than he, which broke the important rule in any sphere of business, that the party with the greater knowledge makes (and deserves) the greater profit.

On a market stall he would still need to price his goods, and his lack of expertise would work against him there too. He discarded this option when he concluded that the time taken in finding and running his stall would delay the enticing moment when he could open the next carton.

He visited an auctioneers. When the expert was finally free to see him, Marshall was surprised and disappointed to be confronted with a young female. She is probably more expert in teddy bears than soldiers, thought Marshall. How can one be a specialist when one is scarcely out of rompers?

'I've drawn up a list of the items I have with me, and the price range suggested in the guide.'

The expert, Celia Wasserman, asked Marshall about the guide. He named it. She appeared non-committal.

'Some experts,' she said, 'draw up and publish catalogues as a means of pricing their own collections.' Marshall was amazed. Celia, who had more than a hint, in her placid blue eyes and unpitted complexion, of a china doll, one of the areas she specialised in, asked to see what he had brought. As Marshall unpacked the soldiers, Celia's eyes were on the brightly coloured little men; Marshall's on Celia. It seemed to him that she was impressed, but he had to admire her insouciance.

'May I ask, Mr Marshall, how you acquired these items?'

'They were left me by my father.'

'Sir James?'

'You have done your homework.'

'He was a collector?'

'Of many things, yes. He believed in the best of everything. He banked at Hoares, he drank Bollinger, he had his suits made at Huntsmans. He married a beautiful woman who died at the height of her beauty.'

'We have a choice,' she said later. 'We could sell the collection complete – perhaps even by private treaty – or piecemeal. I haven't said this to a client since I started work in this temple of delights, but yours is one of the finest collections I have ever seen. It's the condition which is critical; in this case the pieces are immaculate. I am obliged to mention that we shall require your signature to a document asserting your ownership of the goods. It's a formality, of course, but a necessary one in a world in which ugly and unscrupulous people pursue objects of beauty and virtue.'

'Is it really such a jungle, Celia?'

'A jungle is all about survival. Here the motives are more subtle.'

The drawback to taking the auction route was the delay. Celia proposed selling the soldiers at the big Geneva sale, an event that would be anticipated with considerable eagerness 'in the trade'. Marshall, who was anxious to test the efficacy of this technique before consigning other goods to auction, asked about reserves and estimates. Celia named some figures, which reassured him. The reserves would be about two-thirds of the prices mentioned in the price guide. The estimates about a third in excess of the reserves. The total value of the collection was estimated at between £15,000 and £22,000.

Marshall was living in a service flat in a large and pretentious block adjoining Regent's Park. The apartments remained popular during difficult times, because the landlords were especially sensitive to the requirements of the tenants. They were not especially efficient in repairing leaking window-frames, or ensuring that the lifts ran as they were intended to, or servicing central heating, but they were meticulous in other areas. The reception area was always attended by men dressed in the fanciful uniforms of Ruritanian major-generals, who touched the peaks of their astonishing caps to residents and guests. A large oak buffet (Liberty Reproduction Arts and Crafts) was covered with magazines called *Country Living* and *Executive Homes* and *Metropolis*. As soon as these were out of date they were removed (and passed on to the patients at University College Hospital just down the road – what need had they to be up to date?). A display cabinet featured simpering shepherdesses and flat-back highwaymen, the management's vision of the residents' vision of Merrie England. Piped music was kept discreetly low and inhabited the consoling middle range between Brahms on the left and Rodgers and Hammerstein on the right.

'My God,' a visiting American was once heard to remark, 'I came all this way on Concorde to hear *South Pacific* played by singing strings in the middle of Toytown.'

But Marshall's service flat could not comfortably contain

Marshall and the cartons, even though these had diminished, were diminishing and would continue to diminish, and he was fortunate that the adjoining flat came on to the market when he was most pressed for space. He rented it, and moved in at once, leaving the cartons where they were.

It was at this time too that his absences from work began to be commented upon.

Shortly after the delivery of his paper in Stockholm and the death of his father, Marshall was co-opted to work at the Third World Overseas Agency, whence it was just a hop to becoming an under-secretary at the Foreign Office. As an external appointee he was freer than most and continued to hop gazelle-like between departments, landing squarely on his feet. Civil servants found him dependable when he advised them on current economic trends; his stuff was a healthy antidote to some of what emerged from the Central Statistical Office. The official figures were not always inaccurate when they left the Office, but the way in which ministers chose to interpret them often stretched them to the furthest horizons of credibility. There were a great many who preferred Marshall's statistics, which arrived with a genial and thoughtful interpretation, beautifully bound and presented. Those who preferred what he provided became known as Marshall's Men. Marshall was highly thought of in the department. Not as famous nor as flashy as his father, it was claimed on his behalf that he was one of only three people in the country who understood money supply. He always denied making the claim himself, and, if pressed to the limit, refused to identify the other two. How could he, since he had never said such a thing in the first place? Perhaps it was because his father had expressed in his will such a lack of confidence in Marshall's financial acumen that Marshall set himself the task of becoming an acknowledged expert. It was not too difficult, given the mediocrity of those around him. He was promoted to the post of Economic Adviser to a permanent secretary at the Treasury. It was thought inevitable that, barring scandals, he would become a permanent secretary himself as soon as a gap on the rails opened up for him. Blocking his path was the portly figure of Sir Archibald Munro.

Marshall's contributions to the weekly departmental meetings became less and less frequent and his excuses whenever he was absent increasingly haphazard and tenuous. Eventually Sir Archie summoned him to the RAC Club for a swim and a chat.

The gloomy and grandiose surroundings seemed to have been expertly designed to reflect Sir Archie's personality. In a smaller pool his bulk would have seemed offensive; here his corporation had the political correctness of a Roman senator. Once at a think-tank Marshall had sat between the Permanent Secretary and Sir Robert Maxwell. He remarked afterwards that it was like being cast in a dinosaur film.

'I certainly wasn't going to make it to the final reel,' he added.

After a swim and a rub-down Marshall and Sir Archie adjourned to the Members' Dining Room. Over the oxtail soup Sir Archie inquired: 'Something the matter?'

Marshall, misunderstanding, made a sympathetic response.

'Not with me, you fool, with you! Question: what is it?'

'I'm fine.'

'Can usually narrow it down. Trouble with women, trouble with boys, trouble with money, or piles. Any of these ring a bell with you, Marshall?'

'No.'

'Pity you're not married. A good base from which to operate, I've always thought. And when they catch up with you, the little woman standing by you is a most sympathetic line to take. Why not treat yourself to a few months off, Marshall, eh? Go to some concerts, read a book or two, climb a mountain, bugger a friend. I'm sure we could pass it off as compassionate leave.'

'I doubt if I'm in need of compassion.'

'If so, you're the only one who isn't, old man.'

A waitress served Sir Archie with steak and kidney pudding. Irately he called her back.

'Roast *and* boiled,' he said. As she left he looked lubriciously after her. 'What a stern! My God, launch that into the Clyde and you'd flood the country as far south as Carlisle.'

While the Permanent Secretary wolfed his apple charlotte, Marshall admitted that he was considering giving the whole thing up. Archie was so moved that he lowered a Savoy finger untouched to the plate.

'You must be dotty. Don't you want your K? What are you in the Service for? Good God, man, don't you want your pension?'

Marshall had not considered that. He did so. 'Would I lose it all?'

'Not if you retired, I suppose. Some of it though. Bonuses and such. Bad policy, Marshall. Only in cases of extreme indiscipline is the pension at risk and unpunctuality is scarcely that. Have you seen the Ministry at nine a.m.? The place is a morgue. Not much better at tea.'

'What does constitute extreme indiscipline then?'

'Selling information to a foreign power.'

'They're still prepared to pay? The PSBR a week before the rest of the world. My God!'

'I'll have the devils on horseback,' Sir Archie said to the waitress. As she turned to go, he smiled and said: 'Time was I'd have had a quick pinch. Do that these days and they haul you in front of a committee. Not like Italy. Even the nancy boys do it there. As a matter of fact Italians don't pinch, they fondle. Did you know that, Marshall?'

'I'll tell you the problem,' said Marshall eventually. 'I find it hard to continue to do work vital to the country's interests only to find the country is doing the exact opposite of what I said she should do. I find it hard to sit idly by while my statistics are traduced. I like figures, Sir Archie. A satisfactory chart, a well-structured spread-sheet, a competently prepared draft. But what happens to them after they leave me is horrendous. It's like sending unarmed children into battle.'

'Have you considered applying for a transfer?'

'Give up what I do particularly well to take on something I'm unqualified for?'

'Happens all the time. In the Cabinet they call it a reshuffle. Anyway, are you qualified to be idle? Stay on,' said Sir Archibald Munro, replete at last and anticipating a pleasantly drowsy afternoon, 'and I'll support you every inch of the way, as the actress said. Leave, and I'll block both your K and your pension. Take three months' break, old man. Have a scalp massage at Trumpers. The man there's excellent. Take a mistress; Dutch are good, if you don't mind hairy armpits. Commune with nature. OK?'

Marshall thought not.

15

Mr Marshall,
This is not the first tape I have recorded for you. Unfortunately when I came to play that back there was a sort of a hiss and a splutter and then silence. So I've been sitting in my hotel room – the window is wide open so you may be able to hear the crickets, but not smell the amazing smells, as I can. Never mind. They are amazing, believe me, and a good deal better than antiseptic.

Are you interested in details of my journey? I would like to tell you how excited I was at being up, up and away in an aeroplane for the very first time. What's extra special about doing new things is having someone to talk to about them, which is why I thought I'd tell you about everything, not just Marcel and his stamps.

Why don't people want window seats? That's one of the things that really puzzle me. And why do some of the people who do have window seats pull the blinds down? For me coming through the clouds and finding myself above everything was one of the most exciting things that has ever happened to me, and yet nobody else seemed to take a blind bit of notice.

There was a choice of crabmeat or beef olives for lunch. I chose the beef olives because I didn't know what they were, and I was so into new experiences by then that I wanted to have them all. But they were quite boring to tell the truth, Mr Marshall, and I suspect the crabmeat was too, because the man in the seat next to mine – he works for

Reebok, he says, and he has a daughter getting married next month and an allergy to wearing man-made fibres – ordered it and said it was not much better than glorified fish paste.

We were a bit late landing, but it didn't matter as much to me as some of the others, because I only had hand-luggage and didn't have to wait around at that roudabout thing, and I took a taxi into Carcassonne as you told me to do, and phoned Marcel, but he was away so I left a message with I think she was his housekeeper but I'm not quite sure whether she understood the message. I think she said he'd be back on Thursday, but I always get my jeudis and my mardis muddled up, so I'll go along on Tuesday on the off-chance.

The hotel is wicked. Sure, you wouldn't believe the sheets, and the croissants for breakfast were hot and extremely crumbly. I felt a bit as if I'm having a holiday, and then I remembered that I'm not here to have a holiday, so I adjusted my thoughts, and set myself to doing something boring like recording this tape. I've got a whole pile of notes in front of me, so I don't run out of things to tell you, but now I look at them again, a lot of them don't seem worth bothering about. I know you said to tell you everything, but are you really interested in how many sachets of shampoo there are in the bathroom? But I have to say, a bathroom to myself, that's the business.

Now I've said that, I can't actually think of anything else to say, so I'll merely sign off, and leave you with the sound of the crickets, and some of the local lads throwing up in the streets – just like Lahinch.

Are you feeling better? Perhaps getting this tape will help. I'm sure I'll get you your stamps and that they'll be just what you're looking for. I've got your money safe about my person, where even the man from Reebok couldn't find it. Joke! So keep your chin up, and I'll speak to you again ever so soon.

16

*T*he second carton had contained a magnificent collection of saltglaze pottery. A bull with a studded collar and enamelled eyes held his head on one side half quizzically, half threateningly. French poodles with ruffed fur rolls stared ferociously at an ingratiating world. There were puzzle jugs, and tureens, lattices, baskets and chocolate pots. There were a pair of Florence Barlow vases decorated with butterflies and a pair of Bessie Newbury vases in swirling greys and greens, blues and ochres. Each piece had been wrapped in cotton wool and sealed into a cardboard tube. There were seventeen large pieces, and three dozen smaller ones. While he was laying them out on the plain trestle table he had acquired for the purpose, Marshall heard a disturbance at the door of the adjoining flat – his flat. There was a ringing of the bell, and a beating of knuckles on the door panel, then Sylvia's voice:

'Are you there, Marshall? They told me at reception that you were in.'

He said nothing and shortly afterwards he heard her steps retreating down the hallway.

17

Three days after Stacey Anne's first tape, a second cassette arrived. The quality of the recording was excellent, far better than her first effort. Jane handed him the Walkman and picked up her darning.

'Your doxy,' she muttered. Not without difficulty Marshall attached the headphones.

Testing, testing, one, two, three, Mary had a little lamb, one, two, three, this is your Darlin' Girl from Clare, and Monsieur Marcel Oblock sitting in the Café of . . .

Les Deux Pigeons . . . – Marcel's booming voice.

At seven-fifteen on April the eighteenth.

Marcel again: *What you must understand, my dear, is that the stamp issues of any country reflect the personality of its people. The Portuguese are a rather – how to put it? – informal race, so errors and varieties abound in their stamp issues. As for their colonies, they didn't pay their bills until the last moment and so it was inevitable that the mother country would stop providing them with stamps. Which is why there are endless overprints and provisional issues. Encore du vin, garçon. As with your British stamps, the Portuguese started – in July 1853 incidentally – with portraits of their monarchs, Queen Maria, King Pedro, King Luis, King Carlos and King Manuel, and an uglier bunch you would not find on any other country's stamps – and that includes Tonga – but we do not concern ourselves with that, do we, just with the desirable Queen Maria.*

Mr Marshall will be thinking about such matters as reprints and paper and gum (am I not right, my old friend?); What is that old French crook trying to palm off on me, I can hear him saying, but he has no cause to worry, twenty-two stamps, every variety represented, the mint and the used, a quite remarkable cache, I think all would agree.

Have you brought them with you, Mr Oblock?

They are in my rooms, my dear, whither you must in due time accompany me if your employer is to acquire Queen Maria, recessed and embossed, printed in Lisbon, designed and engraved by the redoubtable Senhor F. de Borja Freire. But how about some cassoulet to accompany this wine? And what charming green eyes you have.

So how about that for taking my obligations seriously, Mr Marshall? Aren't you proud of me?

At this point the tape became discontinuous.

'Well?' asked Jane.

'He was correct about the reprints. The whole area is a minefield. If they are as he says they are . . . but between the dealer and the purchaser is a great gulf fixed. The one who sells sees only perfection in what he sells, the one who buys looks only for faults.'

'Not like life at all.'

'I sometimes think we are a long way removed from life, Jane, you and I. We have lived indoor lives.'

'Well, sir, that's no bad thing as I see it. You only have to listen to the news on the wireless. Such pleasant voices, but the things they have to tell us . . . Children torturing children, some of the things one hears, I have to switch them off. Do you want the rest of the tape now? I have a rough idea how it's going to end. In tears, I shouldn't wonder!'

'I'm too tired, Jane. Later, I shall.'

Marshall dreamt of a large tank on the surface of which floated stamps on paper. After a while he would fish them out and peel the paper off. He looked at the stamps more closely.

Each bore a face or a place from the past – a large, ramshackle, turreted house, which was Sapience House where he had attended school from the age of eight, and these were some of his teachers there, embossed, lithographed and recess-printed. On chalk-surfaced and unsurfaced paper, but the condition of each, when he looked more closely, was distressing. Some had perforations missing, others were torn or thinned, a few featured clumsy repairs. How could he make a set out of these? But of course he couldn't. So why was he wasting his time poring over this tank? Because he had no choice. Because he had his instructions.

'No rest for you, Marshall, until you have a complete set. And I want to see them cleaned and properly laid out in that nice new stock book. Is that understood?' The booming voice was his father's, and then Sir Archie's.

The task was hopeless because a complete set would have to include himself, but there were no stamps featuring himself, unless one counted this two-hundred-reis definitive, which had an ugly tear running right across the face. He would never get away with that.

Marshall was awoken by Stacey Anne's replacement just as the dream was becoming alarming. Stacey Anne's replacement was called Amelia Kellogg, and was so thoroughly disagreeable that Marshall wondered whether he was being punished for wooing away the Darlin' Girl from Clare.

'I suppose you've woken me,' Marshall croaked, 'to give me my soporific pill.'

'If I had a five-pound note for every time I've heard that remark – I won't dignify it by calling it a joke – I should be a very rich woman.'

'Where's my housekeeper? She was here when I went to sleep.'

'You could hardly expect her to sit by your bed for six hours, at the same time as keeping house for you.'

'Six hours?' Marshall panicked. If it were true that he was

dying, he could not afford to let six hours slide by him without noticing them.

Amelia Kellogg slid a thermometer into his mouth and, sitting by the bed, took hold of his wrist. You are a very disagreeable woman, Marshall thought, but you have beautiful fingers. Her voice was shrill and grating.

'What would you like for supper?'

The nurse showed him the elegantly printed menu card, which was embossed at the head with a lion rampant, reminiscent of the lion on the Norwegian first issues.

'Gravad lax,' said Marshall, 'and fresh fruit salad. Can you ensure that there are no citrus fruits in it because they hurt my tongue.'

'Just don't ask me to peel the grapes for you. Sir.'

Left alone Marshall fumbled with his Walkman. Why had he gone to such elaborate lengths to ensure that neither Marcel nor Stacey Anne was cheating him? Either she would return with the stamps, or she would not. If she did, he had no doubts that the stamps would be as Marcel described them. Honour among thieves was a myth, of course, but honesty between dealer and collector was essential to both. Marcel was all right. One of the old school. One couldn't mistrust everyone. Life was too short. Auctioneers, now that was a different matter altogether . . .

The tape resumed. Marcel described each of the stamps to Stacey Anne, and she responded non-committally. Then the voices ceased, to be replaced by ominous gasps and rustlings.

Marshall was amazed. At Stacey Anne, at Marcel, and at himself. On her return Stacey Anne would explain that she was a good Catholic girl. That there were things she had dreamt of in Clare (dreams again!) that only became possible in France. That she had not undertaken the commission, he must understand, expressly with the purpose of . . . well, what the hell (she said), I might as well say it since I did it, getting fucked. But that the strangeness of the situation, the foreignness, the luxury, the food, the wine, all that money in cash, and Marcel himself. It was all very seductive to an innocent young girl. Why should Marshall be amazed? At Marcel perhaps, for he had never associated that old crook, that balding, sweaty Frenchman, with such matters. Well, of course, being bald, or sweating, or French, none of these, of themselves, put him out of commission, but the totality of it, well, *were philatelists romantic*?

What was it George Orwell had called stamp collectors? 'A silent fish-like breed.' Then there was a supercilious article he had once read, not in a stamp magazine, but in a superior Sunday supplement, about collectors. It said that stamp collectors were anally obsessed, repressed homosexuals. It questioned why women do not collect and hoard as men do. Because they don't. They like things to be nice, but do they like them to be perfect? The over-educated author thought probably not. (Marshall was not sure what the anus had to do with it.) The article had caused Marshall to consider: amongst the collectors of his acquaintance, how many would he confidently categorise as happy heterosexuals? He could think of none.

But principally when he heard the moans and the gasps on the tape, Marshall was amazed at himself, for he felt an unmistakable twinge of jealousy. He had not supposed dying men had time or energy for such matters. He wanted to make love once more. He wanted it to be as it had been with Jacqueline. He suspected that the food Amelia Kellogg had brought him had not been entirely as described, for, try as he might, he was unable to stay awake.

'Jane,' he said to his housekeeper when she brought in the mail the following morning, 'did you listen to the tape you brought me yesterday?'

'Well yes, sir, I did. I had been instructed to do nothing which might alarm you, and so I thought it best –'

'And you concluded that the tape would not alarm me?'

'But, sir, did it?'

'Not alarm exactly, no. When does the girl get back?'

'This afternoon, I believe.'

'Hmm.'

'There's a letter for you that you ought to look at arrived this morning. It's from the Palace, and I don't mean Crystal.'

'Did you open that one too?'

'They want to make you a knight. That's nice.'

Marshall and Jane had stayed together since the death of Sir Jim. Jane had come to Tall Trees as a kitchen maid when Marshall's father was at Eton; now as an old woman she would see Marshall knighted. She ought to have died before him. It would have been deferential.

'You never ask questions,' he said.

'Not my place to.'

'You're not curious?'

'Not beyond bearing, sir, no.'

'I would be.'

'There's not much I don't know. The rest is private.'

'You don't know why I collect stamps?'

'It doesn't matter,' said Jane. 'People do as they choose. Some do.'

'It's so that after –'

'I'm not concerned with after. It's not my place. But congratulations, sir. I should have said so before. Should I order some champagne? Why did they wait till now?'

'Sir Archie died,' said Marshall. 'That'll be it. At least I saw him off. Bollinger, Jane, I think.'

18

*T*rying to recall when last he had felt sexual jealousy, Marshall remembered Sylvia's first boy-friend.

Sylvia had been seventeen, the boy-friend twenty, Marshall twenty-five. She living still at home, attending the local school, taking her exams, doing well enough, a plain girl with broad shoulders and hips. The sweetness of her smile made – and could still make – Marshall's heart melt. He had come to Tall Trees for the weekend to report to his father on life in the Treasury Office where he then worked. Sir Jim encouraged these visits; he would ask Marshall to 'give me a half-hour of your valuable time' and take him 'for a stroll around the estate'. Marshall was flattered as soon as he realised that his father was intent upon picking his brains. For the first time he had something his father needed – information from the fountain-head. No matter how much he protested that the figures he had to work with might not be reliable, that they were often 'guestimates', that they had not been (and often could not be) checked, the more enthusiastic Sir Jim became.

'What's it matter whether the figures are accurate or not? All that matters is that they are official and that I get them first.'

He told his son the story of how the Rothschilds had cashed in on Britain's victory at Waterloo by employing homing pigeons to bring them the news first. Marshall had heard the story so often that he was becoming sceptical about its veracity. If ever he met a Rothschild – and the chances were that he soon would – he would ask it.

(Later when he did, he did. Yes, they said, we did. They added that there was nothing as valuable as knowledge. He believed them because of who they were. In his heart he believed that a bullet was the most valuable thing in the world. Later he was to learn that a stamp could be. Knowledge gets you money. Money gets you power. Bullets get you killed. Stamps get you nothing, except your letters posted. And yet . . .)

'Yes, father, but a battle is something else. There couldn't have been a great deal of dispute about who won Waterloo. In a battle, the winners are the ones who get to do the looting, I suppose, and are given a turkey dinner when they get home. But with statistics, well, you can make them jump through hoops if you're so inclined, and most of those whom we supply are.'

'I want them pure and unadulterated,' said his father. Like Sylvia, Marshall thought.

As father and son walked between the firs and across the croquet lawn, prickling with spines and cones and thorns, Marshall felt pleased to be useful, but nervous too. He had signed the Official Secrets Act. Did it not apply to his father, Grand Old Man that he was, as much as to lesser mortals? That arm that Sir James placed across his shoulders might be affectionate or proprietary or merely protecting his interests but Marshall did not dare to crawl out from under it. He felt he was being looted. His father was, in other ways too, a looter. As Marshall would, to his great advantage, discover.

When they returned to the house, Sylvia's admirer had arrived from Oxford, Sylvia having invited him to tea.

It was clear that he was no film star. As soon as he walked into a room the room was diminished. He looked studious, and his tangled, brown hair seemed to have been abandoned to fend for itself.

'This is Brian,' Sylvia had announced, colouring slightly.

Brian had just 'gone up' to Keble College, Oxford. He had expressed his intention of inviting Sylvia to a 'commem.'. Sylvia, not knowing what a commem. consisted of, certainly understood 'invitation' and liked the sound of it a great deal. Brian talked at some length about his chosen subject, metallurgy, and, after tea, beat Marshall at chess. When Marshall proposed a return game, Brian thanked him but declined and joined Sylvia in the conservatory. For some time laughter could be heard and, when the laughter evaporated, even more amazingly, silence. Marshall felt that he had lost two games.

At the end of the weekend, Marshall grabbed Sylvia and thrust her into the privacy – apart from the masks of dead animals – of the gun room.

'Are you sure you know what you're doing?'

'What am I doing?'

'With Brian.'

'Not much, yet. More's the pity.'

'I'm not keen, Sylvia, on that sort of remark.'

'Is it any of your business?'

The trouble was not so much Brian – he was the sort of non-potential non-brother-in-law that it was hard to take exception to – but the effect he was having on Sylvia. She announced her intention of going on a walking holiday with him. Offa's Dyke.

'But you don't even like walking. You never walk.'

'A person can change. You do things you used not to do.'

'Have you spoken to father about it?'

'Not yet. But I expect I will. I want to borrow some maps from him.'

'If you don't speak to him, Sylvia, I will. I probably will anyway.'

Marshall's frustrations increased when he discovered that Sir James seemed on the whole indifferent to his daughter's plans.

'It's not as though she gets that many offers. Any offers, come to that. I thought of sending her to Switzerland, but better no offers than offers from the Swiss.'

'Don't you think it's a situation fraught with danger, father?'

'No, not really. I mean Offa's Dyke isn't something you can fall off, is it? Or into. And if you're implying that I should be more concerned with Sylvia losing her cherry, then you're right, but a) the damage may have already been done and b) if not, it's unlikely to happen on a youth-hostelling tour with a first-year Keble student reading metallurgy and c) if it does, he's unlikely to run out on her, or treat her otherwise unkindly.'

A month later Marshall revisited Tall Trees. The Offa's Dyke shenanigans would have taken place by then, but the commem. ball was still a few weeks off. Sylvia was playing a Chopin mazurka on the piano. She played loudly and confidently, wrong notes and all, like a car driven fast up an unmade road.

'How was it?'

'Out of tune.'

'Sylvia!'

'How was what?'

'Offa's Dyke.'

'Fine.'

She did him the courtesy of truncating the mazurka. A weird disharmony throbbed in the air.

'Lovely actually.'

'And you're still friendly with what's-his-name?'

'With Brian? Oh yes. Nice chap.'

'Why didn't you send me a postcard?'

'I did, Marshall. Hasn't it arrived yet?'

He studied her carefully. She was wearing a skirt with a drawstring and a blouse in a particularly hideous shade of mustard. She looked exactly as she usually looked. But then she smiled at him and said teasingly:

'May I go on playing now, or is there anything else you want to know about my private life?'

He left early on the Monday morning, and, finding on the doormat a letter addressed to his sister and with an Oxford postmark, impulsively picked it up and thrust it into the pocket of his overcoat. Weeks later when he collected the same coat from the dry cleaners, it was mentioned that a letter had been found, and he opened it without any recollection of the incident and without glancing at the name on the front.

Darling Sylvia,

We just can't go on like this. If you have any feelings for me at all, meet me on Thursday next at College and we can discuss everything. If you don't turn up I'll know that none of it meant anything to you. I'll be shattered, but life goes on, and mine will too somehow, I expect.

Love
Brian

19

*B*ack from Carcassonne, Stacey Anne seemed like a new girl. Brimming with good health and confidence, she strolled through the corridors of the clinic as if she had just been raised to the peerage. Her progress was the subject of much speculation – and not a little jealousy. She had returned, as she had left, without explanation or excuse, but she walked down the very centre of the corridors and no longer had the look of someone on a weekly wage. She had bought a blouse and a skirt in Carcassonne, and she wore them with élan.

Jane admitted her to Marshall's private room. Shapeless under the covers, Marshall was asleep, his handsome head turned away from the light. He snored slightly and occasionally vented a high shuddering sigh.

'Well,' said Jane, 'at least you came back. Some girls wouldn't have.'

Stacey Anne said pertly: 'I promised to, and I did. I did everything I was supposed to.'

'Just that?'

Stacey Anne looked sharply at the older woman, with amused interest, and without shame.

'So you listened too, did you? Well, well, whatever next? And are ye not going to wake the old fellow up?'

'Have you brought the stamps?'

'What else should I be here for? Mucky little bits of paper I thought them.'

'Leave them with me, Stacey Anne. I'll give them to Mr Marshall as soon as he wakes himself up. No need to detain you.'

'Maybe not, but my instructions stated I was to bring them back to the man himself, so that's what I'm thinking to do.'

Jane could not understand how she had been put on the defensive, but she said: 'Very well,' calmly enough, and folded her hands in her lap. So the two women sat either side of the old man's bed and waited, as women have been accustomed to do.

20

*I*t was the third carton that entirely altered the rules of the game. It contained fewer items than the previous cartons, but they were choice ones. A silver punch-bowl, a mounted egg, a silver tureen, a pair of candlesticks, and a porringer. Marshall sent for Celia Wasserman and confronted her with the silver, which he had removed to his own flat and set out on the dinner table covered with a damask tablecloth, newly acquired from Harrods. The items looked hugely impressive though lustreless.

'I should warn you straight away, Mr Marshall, that I am no silver expert. Toys, dolls, teddies and mechanical ephemera are the extent of my expertise. I get by on pottery and porcelain with a little help from my friends, but I will have to bring in a colleague for the silver.'

'I understand.'

'Talking of which the saltglaze is causing quite a stir. I have had several discreet inquiries from those who are best qualified to pay fancy prices.'

'Good.'

'*Extremely* good, and not that common in these belt-tightening times. These are the pieces, are they?'

'They haven't seen the light of day for many years. I thought it best not to polish them.'

'Sensible of you, Mr Marshall. We had a man with a George II sideboard last week. "Thought I'd just give it a bit of a polish before I brought it in," he said. Burr walnut. Taken the patina right off. Still, there are some who paint their furniture white.'

It was the weight of the silver which was so impressive. The candlesticks grew out of the table like tree-trunks, the tureens swelled like craters. Such confidence of taste! Such arrogance of craftsmanship!

'An extraordinary treasure-house,' said Celia. 'Frankly, I'm out of my league.'

She returned a few hours later with a languid man who seemed scarcely to have the energy to fill out the shoulders of his suit. Everything about him was dishearteningly louche except for his piercing eyes, which missed nothing. Celia introduced him as Judas.

'He has a sister called Lucrezia. His parents were very Bloomsbury.'

Judas wasted no time. He opened a round tin of what appeared to be boot polish and rubbed away at a small section at the base of a tureen. Marshall lit a cigar. Celia felt proprietary.

'Paul Storr,' said Judas at last. It was the first time he had spoken since he entered the flat. '1819. The florid style's entirely characteristic, and there's the mark. There's a companion piece to this in the V and A. And this mounted egg is Augsburg, late fifteenth early sixteenth, silver-gilt. The punch-bowl is German too – Munich. The porringer is interesting. You see that the cover has these three animal heads in place of a finial. That is so it may be reversed and used as a salver. Ingenious and beautiful. 1675 I fancy, though the initials are hard to decipher.' He exchanged a glance with Celia.

'I've heard of Storr,' said Marshall.

From a briefcase as thin as himself, Judas removed a form.

'I've seen those before,' said Marshall, 'but this time I think I

77

should negotiate a more favourable deal. You operate a buyer's premium, don't you?'

Celia said: 'All the main houses do these days. We have no choice.'

'You should call to mind the Gadarene swine.'

'These decisions are made above our heads –'

'My question remains. Why should I pay commission when you are already collecting from the buyer? Would I be wrong to describe the practice as having your cake and eating it?'

'Nice silver,' said Judas.

'Not thirty pieces though.'

'Alas, no. Wonder where it came from.'

'I am prepared to let your company handle the sale of this fine silver,' said Marshall, 'but I am not to be identified in any way as the vendor and I am not prepared to pay your company more than five per cent of the hammer price. The remainder of the premium will come to me.'

Again Celia and Judas exchanged glances.

'And if you're agreeable to that, how about an advance? Shall we say half the estimate for the five items. Why don't we?'

In the taxi Celia asked Judas why he had agreed to Marshall's demands.

'He would have gone to Sotheby's or Christie's. This stuff will make the centrepiece of a very attractive sale. Where's it come from, Celia?'

'He hasn't said.'

'His daddy?'

'Possible. All the previous stuff has been first-rate too.'

'You are to find out as discreetly as you can. If he has come by it nefariously we need to know.'

'But then we couldn't sell it . . . '

'You think not?' said Judas, and put his hand between her thighs, where it frequently rested. 'We can sell anything. We also need to know whether there is more where that came from. If there is then our low commission is a sprat, Celia, to catch a mackerel.'

'Other sprats.'

'Nice one, darling.'

'Where to?' asked the cabbie.

'Twice round the park,' said Judas.

21

*A*nd in the immaculate room of the clinic the two women still sat either side of the dying man, waiting for him to wake.

Jane thought: I have heard the sounds you utter when you are making love, Stacey Anne, and what you shout out, and you are not ashamed that I have heard these things. I know a good deal more about you than you about me – unless he has told you things, and, after all, why should he, and, after all, what does he know? I'm little to him. You're nothing. Only somebody useful to employ on a delicate transaction, somebody whose innocence made them useful . . . but was it innocence I heard on that tape, was it innocence that chose to leave the tape running?

Stacey Anne thought: She is jealous of me, because I am young and can have them if I want them. And she is thinking that she heard me on the tape, and why did I permit it? An' sure an' begorrah, isn't it a great moment in a young girl's loife so, and sure wouldn't she be a mean-spirited young hussy if she kept it to herself? But does she think, because of this, that I would entice him to me too? A dying man, eh? If one could give them life by doing that, why that would be a different matter altogether, but to have dying flesh inside you, no thank you, not my cup of Tetley's at all, at all.

Jane thought: Does she think I haven't had my moments? There were sly glances and whispered invitations, of course there were . . . Even proposed to once, by Mr Clarke who brought the meat every Thursday. He offered me all the meat in the shop. Can't say I wasn't tempted. But who in their right mind would change linen sheets for sawdust and the guests in their fine silks for carcasses? You never know what may be around the next corner, so I hung on. But there was nothing much around the next corner except miles of the same, and after so many years the same begins to have its attractions, as you will discover, Stacey Anne, if you live long enough. Just because I chose to ignore the butchery of Mr Clarke and any others who might happen by, to brush them off, just because I preferred to wait for something a little special – no shame in that. A middle-aged Frenchman with half a litre of cognac inside him, a stranger even, and I didn't hear any sounds of delight coming from him. All very well for a young girl riding him like a rocking horse, or a . . . or a . . .

Stacey Anne thought: Or would I, if he wanted it very much, and was prepared to pay generously for my time? I might. Let's say, for the sake of argument, a grand. With a grand I could get myself smartened up, my hair done in that Julia Roberts way, looks so natural but costs a bomb, and a really nice coat and some really nice undies. The undies so that a girl feels sexy, and a coat so that she looks refined. Peel off the skin, and there are the pips and the juices. I might, for a grand. I might for less than that entirely. A girl might, out of the generosity of her spirit. Although, a dying man . . . ? Be like a worm, would it? Be like a worm, of the earth earthy . . .

And Jane thought, Where did it go, my life, lived for others? What might it not have been if I had lived for myself?

And Marshall lay inert between them, but his dreams were of other times, other women.

22

Marshall was dazzled by the money. He received a large cheque from the auctioneers against ther sale of the silver, and drew out £5,000 in cash. H e needed nothing for his flat, which was elegant just this side of ostentation, but apart from Jane there was nobody with whom to share its delights. He made it his priority to buy some new clothes. One of his colleagues tended to decorate himself with loud ties, and Marshall was impressed until he read a magazine supplement in which it became clear that loud ties were de rigueur for young executives. Another (a bachelor) wore odd socks, but this, it seemed, was an attempt to recapture a carefree youth, long past. Grey suits, polished leather shoes, striped ties – Old Etonian, Garrick or MCC if possible – these were conventional and regarded as important in the tightly schematic world in which he moved. He heard tell that in the BBC, for instance, middle management still affected jeans and cardigans, but such mildly bohemian eccentricities would not be countenanced in the Department.

Marshall determined to branch out. He bought a wide range of fashion and men's magazines and sat down to study them in Fortnum's Fountain. He marked with an asterisk those few retailers who seemed to combine the exuberance he was looking for with genuine style, and set off to do the rounds.

The reality was quite other than the advertisements had promised. The customers, as well as the sales assistants, were half his age, and for the most part black or gay or both. He found himself embarrassed, something for which he was ill-prepared. He glanced in mirrors – there were plenty of these about – and became aware of sidelong glances, eyebrows raised, and half-smiles in which he read pity, even contempt. His father had taken him, while still a boy, to be measured for a suit at Huntsmans; in these shops to have demanded such attention to detail would have seemed absurd. Trousers were baggy anyway, and jackets worn loose. Alert to the prices he was expected to pay, Marshall was discouraged to find that the clothes were rarely made from proper materials, cotton, wool or linen. Far more often the label, if there were a label, spoke of composites which meant nothing to him. Once he asked a loose-limbed sales assistant, who looked as if he had loped straight out of the Harlem Globetrotters, whether a jacket would 'last'.

'What do you mean sir, last?' was the reply.

After two days' serious shopping, Marshall found himself the possessor of two jackets, two pairs of trousers, and a small selection of shirts, ties, socks and boxer shorts. Feeling middle-aged and something of a failure, he made his way to Savile Row for a couple of suits, and some traditional shoes. Later he discovered that when he ventured out in the baggy trousers and the loose jackets, he was the object of a good deal of attention, not all of it favourable. Once he received a wolf whistle from a small group of younger men – most disagreeable.

These excesses had cost him half of his £5,000. They were not what he wanted.

It was late autumn, wet and cold. He put on his loyal old Burberry.

It had taken him a long time to realise how lonely he had become. He had had women, half a dozen in the thirty years since he had lost his virginity in Germany, on a university trip. Seven in all then, not many. The German girl had been drunk, as he had been, in a bierkeller, and had laughed before, during and even, though far less raucously, after. He had thought: Why is she laughing, this is not meant to be the comedy hour. He had kissed her fiercely to shut her up, but she had tickled him and undone his trousers. Then, as she undressed him, and even while he undressed her, she laughed. Nevertheless she had known what she was doing, this thin, brown-haired daughter of an Essen car assembler. Despite the laughter she had done all that was required with an expert efficiency. She must have guessed how inexperienced he was, and how likely he was to come too soon and spoil the broth, and so she had applied herself to helping them both – and had still had time to laugh. Her hands had been cold around his cock, and she had put it where it belonged, and he had found the warmth there comforting as well as exciting. Coming home. But then she had laughed more loudly, and he had hated her for it. Now, whenever he heard that kind of laugh or a gesture that continental students made, which she had made, wringing their hands in front of their chests to indicate 'Phew! Hot stuff!' and blowing on their fingers, he thought of Ingrid, with gratitude and irritation.

For some time after the German Experience, his curiosity sated, he had comforted himself with that combination of guilty masturbation and sentimental longing that most young men, and many young women, enjoy, until the one becomes tiresome and the other unrealistic.

Three of the four women who had inherited him from the German girl he remembered less vividly. One had been enchantingly pretty, but he had been aware, when she had picked him out at a party and instructed him to take her home, that he was a useful convenience for her. She had gone through the love-making procedures with neatness and efficiency, giving him a memorable night of satiety and self-congratulation, but it was no secret that she was, as they said, 'getting even', having discovered that her fiancé, a booking clerk with a travel firm, had betrayed her with a courier. Marshall could recall her flushed face and her pale, perfect body with pleasure, but nothing else about her, not her voice, not her name, nor where she lived.

The next two had also faded into anonymity. Like old photographs left in the sun, their faces could no longer be identified. One, called Charmian, had tiny breasts, or was that Susan? The fourth was Jacqueline.

After Marshall had been walking some minutes in the general direction of Soho, the rain turned to sleet and it occurred to him that he would have been wiser to have planned his strategy more carefully. Where precisely was he making for? He turned up the collar of his coat. What exactly would he do whenever he reached wherever he was making for? He turned into the comforting fug and bustle of a pub. Why had he not stayed at home and made a few telephone calls?

An office Christmas party was in progress. There were jokes about clients, and lay-out, show reels and presentations. Marshall concluded that these were advertising people. He studied the men's clothes with heightened interest. None of them seemed to be wearing the sort of clothes he had been shown, nor the sort of clothes the magazine claimed these sorts of young men should be wearing. They were abysmally dressed, and unbuttoned shirts dangled over unbelted trousers. Their young women, who were sensibly and conservatively dressed, whooped and cackled with glee, as several of the men took to sitting in their laps.

Marshall ordered a brandy, then a second. He had secured a place on a bench close by a blazing fire, and his coat steamed slightly in the heat. He removed it and draped it over the back of the bench. A roar of triumph and astonishment arose as a monstrous machine decorated with spacecraft spewed out

86

money. Two of the women, mistaking him for a competitor or a client, drew him into their group, and asked him questions about his company that bewildered him. When were they going to make up their minds? Who else was in the running?

'Don't be an arsehole,' said one of the men to the young woman who was pestering him most persistently, 'he's nothing to do with the Joyce account.'

'Aren't you?'

'I don't even know what it is.'

'Who do you work for then? Drew, Bloom and Bagley?'

He decided not to deny it. 'My lips are sealed.'

They found this unaccountably witty, and the girls were challenged to unseal them. A very tall young man, with a paper chain caught up in his hair, challenged him to admit something.

'Are you Drew, Bloom or Bagley?'

'I'm certainly not Bagley,' he said, 'but let me buy you a round of drinks.'

'In that case you're certainly not Bloom,' said one of the girls, which gave rise to hoots of raucous laughter.

From then on he was referred to as Mr Drew, and sometimes as Donald. They insisted on him putting money into the monstrous machine, and several of the young men insisted on pressing buttons for him to secure the best chance of getting a return on his investment. Meanwhile he was drinking more brandy, and at one point in the evening handed over to the barman two fifty-pound notes 'for the kitty'. This added to his popularity, and Donald became Don and even 'Donnie Baby'. At one point in the evening he remarked that he had eaten nothing, and somebody handed him a packet of crisps, which he found it impossible to open. One of the young women, whose name, he gathered, was Michelle (or Rochelle? it was extremely noisy in the pub), took the edge of the package in her teeth and tore it open. Then she took a crisp in her mouth and passed it into his. She had small and beautiful teeth. Her breath was scented with gin and he tasted lipstick on the crisp. She sat on his lap and said that she had a brother called Donald who was already a detective inspector and that she didn't mind at all that he worked for DBB, and were there any openings there, or were there likely to be in the near future, for talented copywriters? She was wearing a blue dress with a V-neck, and a locket dangled between her breasts.

'That's pretty,' he said.

'Oh, the locket? Yes, well, it's eighteen-carat.' Trying to open it she chipped a nail. 'Fucking hell!' she said, and he was excited by her uncompromising language.

He took the locket and opened it for her. On one side was a photograph of a rather fierce-looking man, on the other a rather fierce-looking dog.

'Isn't he sweet?' she murmured sentimentally.

'Which?'

Marshall's £100 seemed to last a long time. Brandies appeared in front of him with the regularity of ducks on a fairground rifle range, and were knocked back accordingly. Michelle, or Rochelle, helped him with them and became passionately insistent that he help get her a job – freelance work would do – in DBB.

'It's the only place where imagination is put at the top of the pad; the only agency prepared to *argue* with clients. Is it true you sometimes forbid them to come on a shoot? I'd do anything to work there.'

Marshall was on the point of emphasising – yet again – that he was a civil servant, not an advertising man, but held back.

'Forbid is a strong word,' he said.

The girl was still on his lap and her lips were nibbling at his ear. Most of her associates had either left the pub, or the planet, when she whispered:

'Are you going to take me home?'

'I'll be frank with you, Donald,' she said, as they lay naked in bed, side by side, arms touching, little fingers entwined, replete. 'I'm not looking for a father substitute at all. Most of my friends are my own age, and one of them's a good deal younger. I just like you for yourself, and I don't think age need come into it at all.'

Her small flat was full of photographs of dancers, and space which could ill be spared was taken up by a bookcase of encyclopaedias.

'The body and the mind,' she said. 'I'd like to have a dancer's body and a mind jammed with facts, so I work out regularly at the LA Centre, and I'm reading these – only I'm starting with W to Z, because I reckon most people start with volume one, and I should like to know things no one else knows. Ask me anything you like about Zanzibar and I'll tell you.'

They made love twice, the first time at her prompting, the second time, in the early morning, at his. She was efficient and assured him that 'in bed you don't have to worry about a thing'. Nor had he until then, except that he worried that he was only pleasing himself.

'Fuck me harder, Donald,' she cried, 'harder and deeper, yeah!'

It sounded as though she was recapitulating something she had read in a magazine, or seen on the movie screen. She was. In their first encounter he clung to the sides of the bed, as if to a raft in a stormy, shark-infested sea, and waited for the storm to blow itself out. Later, when she was half asleep, he took his revenge. The only response she made this time was a deep sigh followed by a slow relaxation. Then he saw her eyelids flutter and a smile twitch on her bruised lips. It pleased him absurdly.

She brought him coffee and scrambled eggs in the morning, and watched him eat. She wore a man's dressing gown which, though belted, yawned to reveal her breasts.

'When do you check in at DBB?' she asked.

'What's the principal export of Zanzibar, Rochelle?'

89

She told him that there was no longer any such country and that her name was Michelle; he told her that not only did he not work at DBB but that he never had. Moreover until the previous evening he had never heard of the company. Michelle was not at all pleased. Eating her scrambled eggs with a rare appetite, Marshall said:

'I don't see why you should be angry that I don't do something that I never claimed to do. The truth of the matter is that I work as an under-secretary at the Treasury – except that I'm on extended leave.'

'An *under*-secretary?' she mused. 'That must be about the equivalent of the office cleaner.'

Marshall ordered a taxi and offered to drop her off at work on his way home. In the cab he asked when he might expect to see her again. Bluntly she told him never.

'Why on earth not?'

'You're not my type, Marshall. You're far too old for me, and I like a hunky physique – you know what I mean?'

'I don't know quite how to put this,' he said, taking her delightfully cool and bony hand in his, 'but I am rather a rich man. I have had an exceptional stroke of luck. I would be more than happy to make some sort of an allowance to you, in return for, well, other nights such as the one we have just delightfully spent.'

'Sweetie,' said Michelle, removing her hand and patting his firmly with it to express friendly determination, 'I already have a boy-friend. And he's not badly off. And if I agreed to your proposal I think he would withdraw himself rather quickly to the sidelines. If you work at the Treasury, even as an *under*-secretary, you can appreciate that that might not be in my best interests.'

Shortly thereafter the girl asked the cab-driver to pull up at her office – or preferably a few doors down the street. As she climbed out the driver muttered:

'Quite right, love. He's old enough to be your family

doctor.'

'I heard that,' said Marshall, aggrieved.

'Then I shan't have to repeat it when you get out, will I, sir?'

23

*W*hen Marshall opened his eyes he panicked. He knew neither where he was, nor who he was. There was light everywhere, and at its most intense point what appeared to be an egg. That was all he could make out, a dazzling egg, and around it a mist of light. The light was also heat, for he was lying in a river of fire. Reason returned. The light could not come from an egg; it must come from a bulb, and so, when he was able to focus his eyes, it proved. There was no river of fire running the length of his bed, merely the fire in his blood.

Gingerly he pressed one leg against the other, and the heat was scalding. He lifted a hand to brush the sweat from his eyes – the hand itself was sweating. Stacey Anne moved quickly into action when she saw him move. She touched his forehead, and then, alarmed, took his wrist.

'Has he taken a turn for the worse?' Jane asked, but Stacey Anne's expression confirmed that he had.

'Why are you both here?' Marshall grunted, 'and what about the other one? Have I been asleep long?'

'A few hours, my dear,' said Jane. 'Sleep is quite the best thing for you at the moment.'

'Not this kind of sleep,' said Marshall. He breathed deeply, but for a moment no breath would come. 'Where is the air?'

he asked. Stacey Anne wiped his face with a scented flannel. 'I'm not a flower-shop,' he muttered. He looked at the younger woman. 'Do you have them?'

Stacey Anne said that she did, and Marshall demanded to see them.

'Not now,' said Jane, 'what can you be thinking of?'

'It has to be now,' Marshall said. 'Now or never. It's not just the paper,' he added, 'but the gum and the perforations. And not just that, but the size of the Adam's apple, and the absence of the pendant curl, and the burelage, and the engraver's initials.'

'I'm sure Marcel knows all about such things,' said Stacey Anne.

'Ah Marcel, of course. I remember. He wrote to me . . . you flew over . . . the tape . . .'

'It's my view that you should get some liquid down first, and some antibiotics, by the look of you,' said Jane.

'Now,' Marshall barked, and again even louder: 'Now!'

Stacey Anne produced the stamps from her bag. They were contained in four stock cards, in an envelope, the five- and twenty-five-reis unmounted mint, with varieties, six stamps in all, in one, the same cancelled in the second, the fifty- and hundred-reis unmounted mint, four stamps in the third, and the same cancelled but with the addition of the cancelled copy of the fifty-reis, double impression, in the fourth. Three hundred thousand French francs' worth. The remembrance made him groan.

'You should have bargained with the man.'

'I did as you told me. Aren't they right?' the girl asked anxiously.

'How can I tell with this beastly light blaring down? Where's my lens? How can I see anything under such conditions?'

Struggling to sit up, Marshall fell back on the pillows, the feebleness of his body in sad contrast to the asperity of his temper. Summoned by Jane, Amelia Kellogg burst into the room, and, with a minimum of preliminaries – just a disparaging reference to Stacey Anne's professional ethics – thrust a needle into Marshall's arm, sending the stock cards flying to the ground.

He woke again in the night, the fever considerably abated. A woman he had never seen before was sitting by the bed, reading a dog-eared paperback in the beam from an anglepoise lamp. He felt something cold against his wrist and turned his head to see a needle attached by a strip of plaster. He shivered.

'I'm cold.'

'I'll rearrange your blankets.'

'I'd like to look at them now.'

'The stamps, do you mean?' The woman had a deep, gentle voice. 'Your housekeeper said you might wish to. She brought in a magnifying glass. I'm the new night nurse, by the way.'

'Do they bring you in when the patients are dying?'

'We each have our own areas of speciality. I am known to be reliable. It's a pleasant thing to be known for.'

He took the stamps and the lens with his free hand. It was shaking. That was something else new. His decline was becoming spectacular.

There was the Queen, in profile, embossed, looking left. Designed and engraved in 1853 by F. de Borja Freire. He had done Her Majesty no services. The double chin, the hooked nose, though not so hooked on the twenty-five-reis. The errant curl gave her a touch of whimsicality.

He asked: 'Do you have a pair of tweezers?' and the woman left her post to find some. But even before she returned he knew that neither Marcel nor Stacey Anne had let him down. He took the unused stamps out of their protective windows and turned them over, finding in each case, as he expected, the brownish gum which, amongst other things, protested authenticity. He returned them to their cards.

'Aren't they fine?' he whispered. 'Such colours!' They were reddish-brown, greenish-blue, lilac and pale lilac. 'Such beauty!'

'They are fine,' she said. 'You're a very lucky man.'

'Will you have Jane bring the European albums in the morning? She'll know which. Just ask her, would you?'

'Old Miss Reliable, that's me,' said the woman, and returned to her sensational literature. 'She's pregnant by the doctor,' she confided, 'but she's going to let the young duke believe it's his. That way he'll be brought up a gentleman.'

But already Marshall was asleep.

24

'I couldn't bring all the European,' said Jane crossly, 'it was expecting a lot of me to bring any at all; horrid, heavy things.'

'What are you trying to make me say? That you're a saint and deserve a place amongst the immortals?'

'"Thank you" would have done nicely. Or, "Next time you must take a taxi. I'd be happy to pay for it." I'd rather have a chance to rest my old limbs than be sanctified.'

'You should have taken a taxi, Jane. Of course I would have paid. Now would you find and send to me that admirable young woman who brought me the Portuguese stamps? I need to thank her in person.'

'*She* gets thanked, does she?'

'Just fetch her.'

Stacey Anne appeared harassed. She was no longer welcome in the clinic, and it had been made very clear that, having burnt her boats there, she should no longer be bobbing about on the waves. She told Marshall that he seemed better, and asked whether the Portuguese stamps were what he had been looking for. He said that they were everything that Marcel had promised, better than he could have anticipated.

'You may help me put them in the place I have waiting for them, Stacey Anne.' He pointed to an album, which she brought over to the bed and placed on an invalid tray. Reverentially he turned the pages; all were filled, until he came to the two set aside for Portugal. He gave her the tweezers and showed her how to insert the stamps, the mint on the first page, the cancelled on the second.

'They're only bits of paper, but they look quite pretty, the way you set them out,' she grudgingly admitted.

'Quite pretty, Stacey Anne? You might as well call Castle Howard quite handsome.'

'If ever I'd seen it I'm sure that I might.'

'It's the colours, you see. When you look at the trials and the proofs, you can see the trouble they took, the designer and the printers, to get things just so. It does them a disservice to shove the stamps haphazardly into a stock book. The way some people treat them, why, it's on a par with the way they treat their wives and children. So I've heard.'

Unable to find any other blank pages, Stacey Anne asked: 'Is it finished then?'

'This album is.'

'There's others?'

'Thirty in all.'

'Thirty?'

'And twenty-eight of them are complete. Faroe Islands and Mauritius are all that are left. Faroe Islands are just a nuisance, but Mauritius is the stumbling block. They are amazingly rare. We could be talking about up to a million pounds.'

'That's not possible,' said Stacey Anne, 'for bits of paper.'

'Weight for weight they are worth more than anything in the world. Much more than gold or platinum. More than plutonium.'

'Would you credit it? And what will you do with them when they're all complete?'

Marshall breathed heavily: 'I shall leave them in perpetuity to the British Museum. They will be exhibited in my name, the Marshall Collection, in display cases, lit from within.

Students and enthusiasts will be permitted to view them. They will remain complete and perfect for all eternity.'

'Eternity? Isn't that something though?'

25

Marshall had quarterly meetings with Arthur Winepress, at which meetings Marshall's financial matters were discussed. Arthur had checked with Jane whether the scheduled meeting should take place and Jane had conferred with Marshall. The upshot was that Arthur was to visit the clinic and hold the accustomed and comforting discussions.

Arthur was little changed from the country solicitor who had supervised the Grand Old Man's will. Marshall had dismissed Battersby and taken Sylvia's adviser as his own. Sylvia had triumphed; whether or not it was down to Battersby's incompetence and Winepress's astuteness, Marshall preferred to be part of a winning team. Although Arthur Winepress had a complexion slightly more florid and a Gladstone bag slightly shabbier than in the old days, although his smelly old retriever had been replaced by another smellier and older, the solicitor still beamed genially on the world, as though expecting the best of it. If his life had been touched by the harsher realities, there were no indications of it – until you noticed the rusting dent to the nearside wing of his Ford station wagon.

He had brought with him a bag of apples.

'Coxes. From the garden. My wife said, "Take him some plums, apples take a lot of chewing," but the plums aren't up to much frankly, and an unripe one can play merry hell with your insides. How are you feeling, by the way?'

'Rough.'

'What a place to feel rough in though! I must say I almost envy you. Who's paying? PPP?'

'They were. Now I am.'

'We are, eh? Well, you've not a lot to worry about on that score, Marshall. It's true that the stock market's looking a little green about the gills, but your portfolio is still broadly based, and you've made quite a killing in Hong Kong.'

'What am I worth?'

'On paper? Well, at the end of last quarter, about six hundred and seventy K, plus whatever you've got salted away in banks that you haven't told me about.'

'It's not enough.'

'Not enough for what? It would be enough for most people. I'm sure your poor sister would be satisfied with a tenth of that.'

'I need you to realise my assets, Arthur. I want everything so I can get at it in a hurry.'

'Is that entirely sensible? I mean I can extricate you from most of your commitments, but what about the long-term stuff? Have you thought about the capital gains tax you'll be faced with? And surely you wouldn't want me to cash in the life insurance policies? I mean, with the greatest respect, Marshall, would that be timely?'

'Well, maybe not the policies, but everything else . . . '

'Very well. But it makes me sad to think that you, of all people . . . The fabric of our society, Marshall, is being torn in pieces, the Church ordaining women, the heir to the throne living apart from his wife and children, scandals in high places – you haven't been foolish in that way, have you?'

Marshall managed a smile. He hadn't, no. Not more than most, nor as much as many. But the cost of the clinic, and the stamps . . .

'Ah, the stamps.' Arthur picked up one of the albums and opened it at The Netherlands. King William III in a decorative frame. Blue, red and orange. Loud and clear. 'Magnificent. Quite magnificent.'

26

After the Paul Storr silver, the remaining cartons might have seemed an anticlimax. But such was the superb quality of their contents, so grandiose the scope of the collection, that Marshall never felt let down. There were surprises. One carton contained nothing but armorial plates, Bavarian mostly, but each of the thirty-five plates (one was in pieces) featured a different coat of arms. One contained wineglasses, dark and austere in their leaded simplicity. One, examples of French animalier bronzes. These pleased Judas particularly. He liked things to be weighty, detailed and signed.

Celia Wasserman took naturally to sleuthing. She was thorough, but she was slow. Judas had set her a straight-forward series of questions:

'Where do Marshall's treasures come from? Are there more and, if so, how many? Is he entitled to sell them? How can we ensure that he does not take them elsewhere?'

She went first to Somerset House and applied for a copy of Sir James Marshall's will. This could not have been simpler. Sir James had left everything – with the exception of a few insignificant bequests – to his daughter. An old *Who's Who* suggested that Sylvia had married Jack Langley. The telephone directory for Central London named nineteen Langleys who bore J as a first initial. Celia telephoned each and asked to speak to Sylvia. The seventeenth call was answered by a well-spoken woman who said:

'Sylvia speaking.'

'I'm a friend of your brother's. Can I speak to you on a rather sensitive matter?'

Sylvia telephoned Marshall.

'Does the name Celia Wasserman mean anything to you?'

Marshall thought fast. If Sylvia knew that he was selling the family silver, even though it was his to sell, it might make her unhappy, discontented, troublesome. Better to lie and save her any distress.

'No.'

'Strange. She claims to be a friend of yours. In that case I shall have nothing to do with her.'

That night Sylvia discussed the curious affair of the friend who was no friend with Jack. Jack was polishing his shoes, a ritual he performed every night religiously, for he polished his shoes as others say their prayers; if my shoes are clean and bright then everything will turn out right. As with most prayers, shoe-polishing proved ineffective. Jack's affairs went from bad to worse as his toe-caps glistened.

'I look at it this way,' said Jack. 'If she says she's a friend of Marshall's, and Marshall says she isn't, somebody is telling porkies, and who has the most to lose from telling the truth?'

'I've no idea,' said Sylvia, 'and I don't much care. Do come to bed, Jack. You're making little sense and you smell of Cherry Blossom.'

'Did she leave her number?'

There were nineteen J. Langleys in the phone book, but only one C. Wasserman. Jack dialled the number early the following morning and told Celia that he was Marshall's brother-in-law, and perhaps he could be of some assistance. They met in an Italian café, near Celia's place of work. Jack ordered glutinous custard tarts sprinkled with nutmeg, and cappuccino for two.

'Your brother-in-law,' said Celia, 'has some beautiful things.'

'Really?' Jack wiped away a custard moustache with a paper napkin. 'Best custard tarts in London, these. If it were left to me to market them . . . But tell me more, Celia.'

'Well, I rather hoped you or your wife would tell *me* more. Whence cometh these treasures? From Sir James's estate, do you suppose?'

'You're not a friend of Marshall's at all,' said Jack. 'Who are you?'

Celia explained about herself and about the cartons, and added, exaggerating somewhat: 'Auctioneers these days have to be whiter than white.'

'Often thought I'd have made a good auctioneer myself.' He tapped his knife on the table-top. 'Sold to the young lady with the seductive smile. What do you think, Celia?'

'A natural gift for it.'

'Well, if you find yourself desperate one day, give me a buzz. Now in answer to your question, Sir James left everything to Sylvia, my wife.'

'So, if Marshall didn't inherit these items legitimately . . .'

'I'll speak to my wife about it. It's not the value of the items themselves,' Jack added, wondering what sort of figures were involved, and how many noughts, 'it's the principle of the thing.'

'I would be ever so grateful if you would speak to Sylvia. It's most awfully kind of you to take so much trouble.'

The next night in the bedroom Jack abandoned his polished praying and instead asked Sylvia: 'Did Marshall inherit *anything* from your father?'

'Well no, nothing. Except a few old boxes from the loft.'

'A few old boxes? The bugger! He's been selling them off at auction and making a tidy packet. Is he entitled to them?'

'We had a sort of informal understanding.'

'How informal? Informal enough to impress a court of law?'

Sylvia called on Marshall. She was wearing her most formidable two-piece. Only a few of the choicest treasures from the adjoining flat were on display in Marshall's place.

'To what do I owe this pleasure?'

'Yes, it should be a pleasure, shouldn't it? Brothers and sisters. But we're drifting apart.'

'I'm not, Sylvia. I haven't budged.'

'You've not played entirely fair with me, Marshall.'

Marshall remembered a letter in an overcoat pocket, an intense young student from Keble College.

'Haven't I?'

'These sales of treasures from the loft at Tall Trees.'

Marshall glanced sharply at his little sister, who seemed assured and confident, despite playing away.

'A few knick-knacks is all,' he said.

'You knew, Marshall, didn't you? Ever so casual. House clearance! I'm not even sure they are yours to sell. But if they are and since you are selling them, I want a part of it.'

'"I want" never gets. We had an agreement. You got the house and all the money. God knows what you did with it all. Or should I say, "Jack knows"?'

'Jack has his problems.'

'The truth of it is, as you well remember, that in return for the knick-knacks I agreed not to contest the will. There's not a court of law in the country would feel you were the victim of sharp practice. The house, the furnishings *and* the money against a few old boxes. I've never been ill-disposed towards you, Sylvia. No more am I now. And if you were in serious need . . .'

'It's not the need, Marshall, it's fairness.'

'Well exactly. And Father was more than fair to you, as you very well know. This is a nonsense, Sylvia. It won't run for you.'

Marshall made a date to take Celia Wasserman to lunch.

There were restaurants in Covent Garden then, all lemon-and-lime wash, and yucca trees in Casa Pupo foot-baths. Marshall took Celia to one of these. She thought it very elegant, and said as much, as the waiter, dressed in matador pants, brought two large plates containing seven broad beans, three asparagus spears and what appeared to be a puddle of motor oil.

Marshall waited while Celia became thoroughly engaged with a délice de pigs' trotters (or something of the sort) then covered her manicured hand with his.

'It was foolish of you to betray me like that,' he said. Celia's response was accurately predicted by Marshall.

'I don't understand. What can you mean?'

'You contacted my sister. You cast doubts on my integrity and caused trouble between us. I had hoped that our relationship was worth more than that.'

Celia pushed her plate to one side. The food had lost what little flavour it had once possessed. 'I just wanted to be sure. The things you were giving us were of such unusual quality. It was natural that we should want to take elementary precautions before –'

'Before nothing. You should have raised your doubts with me in the first instance.'

'Yes, I should.' With a desperate gesture Celia squeezed Marshall's hand twice. 'An apology is in order.'

'More than an apology. Or, alternatively, sleep with me.'

'So, sleep with him,' said Judas. 'If you work out just what we'll be saving in commission on the sales we're so far committed to (let alone any future ones) it'll make you the best-paid whore in London.'

'And you the best-rewarded pimp.'

Judas had a friend who was expert in animalier bronzes. Judas invited his friend to a private view of Marshall's collection. The friend, Jules, was impressed and intrigued. He ran his manicured fingers over horse and dog and Shetland pony and, in a parody of lascivious approval, smacked his lips.

'Succulent,' he said, 'and well done, Judas.'

'*Quite* well done,' said Judas, 'actually. Because although we do have the stuff to sell we get minimal rewards for doing so.'

'How odd,' said Jules, who sold coffee futures in the City. 'What a curious way of doing business. I sell what doesn't exist and make profits from it, and you make no profits from selling what does. It's remarkable that we're both still around to be eating such delectable chow.' (For they were eating in Jules's Eaton Square flat, and Jules had splashed out at Harrods gourmet counter). 'As a matter of interest I've met one of these pieces before. It was part of the Auerbach Collection. A Munich collector. He had an exhibition in the Thirties and I've got a catalogue at home. This is the piece: "The Cossack's Adieu". He directed Judas's attention to a cossack sitting on a disgruntled-looking horse while kissing his girl-friend. Eugene Lancerre 1848–1886. Nice work. Long tail, hasn't he? The horse, that is. The other pieces could be from Auerbach too, but this one had a full-page illustration in the catalogue.'

'Could it be a copy, Jules?'

'Nah. Do me a favour. I know about coffee and I know about bronzes. What do you know about, Judas?'

'Not a lot. Silver. The market-place. Beardsley a bit, but I am about to become an expert in a wholly new area.'

'Tell me.'

'I'll tell you in bed.'

'Heigh ho,' said Jules, 'bang bang bang. Here we go again. It's like being back at school.'

'My new area of expertise,' said Judas an hour later as he broke off from kissing his friend's unresponsive chest, 'is going to be Auerbach.'

'Auerbach,' Judas told Celia a week later, 'owned all the bronzes. He was a Bavarian industrialist who made rolling stock for the German railways. Probably made those notorious cattle-trucks which were used to cart his family, his friends and himself to Bergen-Belsen. Carrying collaboration too far. His daughter survived. She came to England in 1938 on a special scheme set up by a Jewish charity in London. Children who were thought to be at risk could come to England if they could identify a home to come to. The scheme was a bit surreptitious given the rampant anti-Semitism in Whitehall at the time. It needed a friend in high places to oil the wheels. According to Lloyd George's memoirs, Sir James Marshall was that friend. Wheel-tapper and shunter.'

'And the daughter?'

'She lives in Israel. Don't suppose she knows a thing about all this. Poor love. Interesting, huh?'

'You betcha,' said Celia. 'Shall I set up another meeting with Marshall?'

'I think that would be highly appropriate. Take him to Tante Claire. I'm sure expenses will stretch to that. You're certain he prefers women?'

'A girl can tell.'

'Will you sleep with him?'

'Shouldn't think so. He's far too old. Anyway what business is it of yours?'

'Of ours, my darling, of ours.'

Meanwhile Marshall took the precaution of summoning Arthur Winepress to a meeting at which he told the country solicitor of the informal arrangement he had had with Sylvia concerning the cartons.

'It's possible, but unlikely, that she may bring an action against me for the proceeds of the sales of the items contained within the cartons. I believe Jack is behind it. Were she to do so, would you act for me or for my sister?'

'I hate wills,' said Winepress. 'They bring misery to all concerned, and especially surviving siblings. It was my view at the time that the old boy had treated you a bit harshly, so if

Sylvia approaches me I shall advise her against litigation.'

'Stout fellow,' said Marshall, and then hoped that the solicitor would not be offended.

27

*T*here was just one carton remaining, and Marshall approached it gingerly. He had played fair. He had opened them in whatever order fate (or the porter at the apartment block, who had been well rewarded for his efforts) had placed them, and he had never once anticipated what the next box might contain. But he delayed opening the final carton for two weeks. His life would be the poorer when there were no more surprises wrapped in cotton wool and tissue awaiting his attention. He had become thoroughly organised. Having opened a carton he would take a representative sample to the Victoria and Albert Museum, or wherever a collection of similar items was to be found. He would buy a specialist book or books on the subject and immerse himself in details of firing and casting, glazing and carving, engine-turning and engraving. Only when he had satisfied himself (as far as was possible in the time he made available) as to authenticity and provenance would he betake himself to Celia Wasserman, or occasionally, when common sense suggested it, some other dealer or auctioneer.

Marshall became known in many of the best houses, and was immediately ushered into a private room at several of the most highly respected dealers. People were intrigued. He always sold and never bought. Unless he had agents working for him, he could scarcely be a dealer himself. He was knowledgeable about pieces but not about prices. He always demanded 'fairness'. He did not always look for the best possible price, but he was determined not to be exploited. Some wondered whether he was a high-class fence; but it was in nobody's interest to imply as much. It was fervently hoped that the supply – wherever it emanated from – would never dry up. In time it had to.

There was a sense of occasion about the opening of the final carton. Marshall sent Jane off in a taxi to visit her only living relative – her niece, whom she detested. The flat which had housed the cartons was now almost empty; only Marshall, the last cardboard box, a bottle of vintage champagne, and a glass. He speculated about the contents.

There had been no duplication in the other cartons. All the items had been small, all of the finest quality, but the selections had been idiosyncratic. One box had contained several dozen meerschaum pipes, carved in Vienna with amber mouth-pieces. He had taken several to the curator of the Bragge Collection at the British Museum. The curator had lovingly fingered a pipe carved with sea monsters and explained that the word 'meerschaum' came from l'écume de mer, or sea foam, because the silicate of aluminium from which the bowls were constituted resembled petrified spume. The curator's advice to Marshall about how best to market the pipes resulted in successful sales, and Marshall invited the curator to keep a pipe for his collection. It was there when I last visited the British Museum.

Another carton contained a quantity of duelling pistols beautifully cased in matched pairs with compartments for all the accessories. Another was filled with flutes, another with sporting trophies, another – to Judas's delight – with spoons. There were no bills of lading, receipts, dockets or evidence of any kind. The wrapping, the cartons themselves, gave nothing away.

So to the final carton. A large number of black books appeared, and then a larger number of brown envelopes. He opened an envelope. It was full of stamps. He examined one at random. It was olive green and was inscribed 'Pakke-Porto' across the top. Then, above a symbolic representation of a stormy sea and below a pattern of flying gulls and a crown, was depicted a polar bear erect within a cartouche. As Marshall was later to discover, this was the Finnish one-öre Parcel Post first issue of 1905, highly desirable and well catalogued at £225. He opened one of the black books. Within strips of cellophane were secured hundreds of stamps. One book seemed devoted to each of the major countries. Confident that these stamps, like all the other treasures, would be of the finest quality, Marshall telephoned for a taxi-cab to take him to the Strand, where some of the greatest philatelic experts in the world set up their stalls.

'I don't want expert advice. I don't want to sell just now, or to buy. I have stamps. What I am after is the paraphernalia necessary to put my stamps in order.'

'We have a useful beginner's pack here, sir, reduced from fifteen pounds to a highly competitive twelve ninety-nine. What do you get for your money? A simplified all-world catalogue, a stock book, a magnifying glass and a pair of tweezers. Albums and mounts are available separately, sir, but we don't entirely recommend mounting stamps by the use of hinges any more.'

Displeased by the use of the word 'simplified', Marshall moved on and, advised by a friendly customer who had overheard the exchange, found himself in a basement in Covent Garden, surrounded by stacks of accessories of every kind.

'Let me put it to you this way. I want the best, and I want all that's necessary. I want it delivered to my apartment tomorrow, the earlier the better. I shall leave you an open cheque. Here it is, with my address on the back. When you send me the goods you will kindly include an itemised receipt. Good day.'

Marshall spent the rest of the day in the London Library and visiting the National Collection in the London Museum. He was unaware of the passing of time, and was amazed to find himself late for his appointment with Celia.

Seen from a distance Marshall and Celia were like two ducks pecking at waterweed. When one head turned downwards the other stayed up, alert to danger. A warier pair of diners could not have been found in that popular restaurant.

'Uncovered any more treasures in your Aladdin's cave of delights?' Celia inquired.

'Stamps.'

'Don't know much about stamps.'

'Nor I.'

Celia sipped at her mulberry-red wine, and relished both it and her power over this powerful, older man. 'Good news about the bronzes,' she said. 'Judas has a friend who is a real old-fashioned God-fearing expert, the sort of fellow to go into the jungle with where bronzes are concerned.'

'And he likes mine?'

'Like is hardly a strong enough word in the circumstances. He relishes them. He also –' and Celia pierced a thin slice of duck with one prong of her fork, a gooseberry with another – 'recognises them.'

The weightiness with which Celia delivered these two words alarmed Marshall, as it was intended to.

'How can that be?'

Celia explained how that could be, and left a pause in which Marshall could, if he wished, respond. Wisely, though disappointingly for Celia, he said nothing.

'You really knew nothing of this?'

'No.'

'This woman in Israel – I suppose she might have a claim to the bronzes, and other items, if they all came from her father.'

'Yes,' said Marshall. 'Complicated though, as these matters

usually are when records are non-existent, or destroyed, as in the cases of so many of these concentration camp victims.'

'To sum up,' said Celia, 'let me suggest that we should agree to keep quiet about the whole Auerbach connection.'

'Why not?'

'Judas will be pleased, Judas's friend will be pleased, you will be pleased, and the heiress will be no worse off for knowing nothing.'

'True.'

'You will have to sign some carefully drawn-up indemnity forms, of course, and I see no reason to change our existing commission agreements.'

'None.'

'And I shan't go to bed with you, Marshall. According to this month's *Marie Claire*, older men are "out" just now. I have to get myself a toy-boy as an accessory apparently. But there's good news too.'

'What's that?'

'The meal is on Judas.'

28

*T*he albums were important. Marshall had considered the possibilities for some time before paying a visit to Quaritch, the book dealer. Marshall signed the visitors' book which was weighty with American academics, and asked to see a senior partner. Ensconced in an office with an elderly man whose demeanour was encouragingly sombre, he looked around him at yards of Morocco and vellum, framed by mahogany and fronted by glass.

'In the early days of stamp-collecting,' Marshall explained, 'due regard was paid to the presentation of a collection. Bound in art cloth on strong bevelled boards, the pages of an album might be of semi-cardpaper, lithographed in the quadrille ground and border, and topped and tailed with marbled endpapers. The whole thing would be leather-bound, as often as not, with a monogram tooled in gold. The albums might then be secured in slipcases. The early Stanley Gibbons "King's Own" albums were objects of distinction, and even the hugely successful Ideal range had its own dignity.'

'You are speaking, sir,' said the old man, 'to a philatelist of many years' standing, a regular exhibitor at the RPS, and an erstwhile silver-medallist. I am impressed with your grasp of the subject, but why do you not explain your precise needs, so that I may see best how we can accommodate you?'

The skin of the elderly man was the colour of tanned leather, and a musty smell emanated from him. Marshall felt inclined to lay him flat and blow the dust off him.

'Very well then. My collection is a collection of first issues. I ignore pre-payments, labels, wrappers and such vulgarities to concentrate on adhesives, beginning, of course, with Britain's Penny Black issues, then chronologically taking in the Swiss Cantons, the Brazil Bullseye stamps, the American Confederate States and so on. I have made an arbitrary decision to draw a veil on any stamps issued for countries created after 1960. One has to stop somewhere, and many of the more recent countries to issue stamps are spurious in their constitutions and fraudulent in their intent.'

'Even without those Johnny-come-latelies we are talking about a great many countries, sir.'

'Indeed we are, but bear in mind that I am only concerned with the first issues of each. Two pages then per country, one for the first issues mint, one for the same stamps cancelled, and all set out chronologically, as it might be: volume one 1840 to 1850, taking in Mauritius, the USA, Bermuda, Bavaria, Belgium and France as well as those aforementioned. Plus, in 1850 itself, Austria, Austrian Italy, British Guiana, Hanover, New South Wales, Prussia, Saxony, Schleswig-Holstein, Spain, Switzerland and Victoria. The second volume would cover maybe the twenty-eight countries which issued between 1851 and 1854; thereafter as required.'

'The paper I take it should be of the finest and toughest quality; but how do you intend the stamps themselves to be displayed? In Hagler strips?'

'Something of the sort. Stamps, I believe, look their finest against a black ground. No hinges of course. And the binding must be suitably impressive.'

The dilapidated book-man toddled to a cabinet. 'A glass of port, perhaps? You have posed a most interesting question, and I should like to give it the consideration it deserves. A glass

116

of tawny will do us both good and enable me to concentrate my mind.'

A week later over a second glass of tawny Marshall was presented with Mr Harwood's proposal.

'I considered materials first, vellum or buckskin, calf or embroidery, then designs. A fine olive-green morocco, or a Houlden "mosaic". The classicism of Athenian Stuart or James Scott's rococo styles. And do we wish to commission a pastiche or boldly go into the brave new world of modernity? In the end I took 1840 as my clue. What I would be happiest to provide for you is this!'

Abruptly, and with a fine sense of theatre, Mr Harwood removed a linen cloth from a small rosewood table on which lay thirty volumes in morocco-backed cloth, red-brown as clay.

Marshall picked up a volume and opened it. The frontispiece announced: 'The Morbid Anatomy of the Human Uterus'. It had been published by the Med. and Chir. Soc. of Aberdeen in 1835. Mr Harwood, who had a homely West Country burr to his voice – was it innate or acquired? – told Marshall not to concern himself with the contents.

'I'll be glad to shred the beastly things, but to find these boards – and look at the quality and condition of them, just look! Contemporary, and thirty of the buggers; well, your stars must have been shining brightly when you came to Golden Square, Mr Marshall.'

'And the cost?'

Mr Harwood looked disappointed. 'I never discuss money, Mr Marshall. I leave that to my more mundane colleagues. Their lives are orchestrated to the campanology of cash registers. They even take American Express.'

Expensive as they proved to be, the albums had been a happy purchase for Marshall. Their anonymous appearance – possibly to discourage curious young folk from investigating further – was a distinct advantage, except that it was impossible to identify the volumes without opening them. But they were stacked chronologically on his shelves, and in time Marshall was able readily to identify them by tiny idiosyncracies.

29

'*I* want you to help me with a codicil to my will, Arthur. It's to do with the stamps. Let me tell you first about the Ferrari sale.

'Monsieur Ferrari de la Renotière, born in 1848, was Italian by birth. His mother was the Duchesse de Galliera, one of the richest women in Europe. Indeed she owned most of the bits of Europe which were worth having. His adopted father was an Austrian nobleman, whose house in the Rue de Varennes in Paris was left to the Austrian government as an ambassadorial residence, on condition that Ferrari retained the personal use of one wing. There with brief interruptions he lived until 1916, amassing a stamp collection the like of which the world had never seen. In 1916 he went to Switzerland on holiday, but the French government forbade him to return. The bulk of his collection in the Rue de Varennes was sequestered by them, and sold in a series of fourteen auctions between 1921 and 1925.

'However before the auctions could take place, Ferrari, now living in Geneva, instructed Edward Mahé, his secretary, who was still in Paris, to send him many parcels of selected stamps, and these formed the basis of his new collection. This too was sequestered by the Swiss government while a debate raged as to the ownership of the stamps.

'The Ferrari auctions at the Hôtel Drouot realised twenty-six million francs, or four hundred and two thousand, nine hundred and sixty-five pounds at the existing rate of exchange when the pound was worth forty-six and a half francs. Stanley Gibbons had organised a consortium of businessmen in London who had offered fifteen million francs, pre-sale, to the French authorities. It is interesting to note that a buyer's premium of seventeen and a half per cent was imposed for the auction. Nothing new under the sun.

'Ferrari's newly formed collection was bequeathed to the Berlin Postal Museum.

'Now, Arthur, I do not want my collection to be dispersed on my death. I want its uniqueness to be recognised and its completeness to remain intact. No other collection that I have seen can boast both the North Borneo and the Mauritius issues. I have North Borneo. I have yet to acquire Mauritius, which is why I need my cash.

'When I die, you are to see to it, as my executor, that my stamps, which have never been exhibited in their entirety, are lodged in the National Collection, where they should be housed in a special room, named in my honour. As part of the deal I am sure that the state will waive all death duties.

'Arthur, you will leave me now. I am exhausted. Will you come and see me again soon, and let me know whether my plans find favour with the bureaucrats? Thank you for the apples. I shall have one later, if I'm up to it.'

'You're a good chap.' Arthur paused. 'Despite what they say.'

Part Two

1

Six months before the death of his father somebody at work told Marshall that *The Times* was running contact advertisements in its personal column. Marshall was partly amused and partly shocked. *Times* readers – whatever next? The following Saturday he perused the classified section with care. Many of the advertisers referred to a long-term relationship, and quite a few of the possibles kept themselves off Marshall's probables list by mentioning vegetarianism, long country walks and foreign travel. Beauty, youth, good health, tolerance and a fondness for sexual shenanigans were what Marshall was after. Not unreasonable, he thought, but would *The Times* agree to insert an advertisement couched in those terms? An agency promoted its services 'for professional people', and Marshall made an appointment to see them.

Despite the up-market address, Marshall was unimpressed with the premises of the Beauchamp Introductions Agency. It was all very well to have scattered around the outer office magazines of *Interior Design* and *Country Living*, but the only evidence that any designer had been near the Beauchamp Agency itself was a wrought-iron grille between incumbent clients and somnolent staff. This grille invited thoughts of the confessional. When you penetrated Mrs Paget's sanctum sanctorum, you were regaled with Regency chairs, but the framed wedding photographs on the walls were neither Regency nor recent and Mrs Paget's Peter Pan collar was gruesomely prim and proper.

'You must be Colonel Wagstaffe,' Mrs Paget suggested with aplomb. 'Are you a tea or a coffee drinker, or we can run to decaff.'

'I can't answer for Colonel Wagstaffe, but speaking for myself I am a coffee drinker. However I had one with my lunch, and would rather get straight down to the matter at hand.'

'Admirable,' Mrs Paget commented in an abstracted manner before calling to Shirley in the outer office. Shirley came in and stood chewing gum by the door jamb.

'Shirley, why is this gentleman not Colonel Wagstaffe?'

Surly Shirley found this question too philosophical to be easily answered.

'Dunno.'

'Well I "dunno" either, but I would be grateful if you could find out. You'd better bring me another form.'

'Before we fill out any forms,' said Marshall, 'I think we'd better see whether I am wasting my time.'

'Wasting it? Surely not. What else would you be doing with it if you were not with us?' This question from the redoubtable Mrs Paget also proved to be a conversation stopper. 'But you are here, aren't you, and the onus is on myself as the agency's representative to ensure that your time isn't wasted. Match and dispatch is what we try to do, and it's no idle boast. We matched a duke last year, you know.'

'Which one?'

Mrs Paget fluttered a hand vaguely in the air. A silk handkerchief, one end of which was secured within a ring, made colourful arabesques around her head.

'He has connections with Palma, Majorca, and is an excellent bridge player. More than that it would be indiscreet to say, except that he was matched with a lady who is

Something in Cosmetics.'

'I don't believe a word of it.'

'Shirley, we have a cynic in our midst.' Shirley in the outer office showed little interest in this unusual event. 'But to me that is not so much a stumbling block as a healthy challenge. A cynic is an unredeemed romantic.' Mrs Paget straightened her papers on her desk, and Shirley brought her a clean one to add to the pile.

'Name? I can hardly put down "Not Colonel Wagstaffe", can I?'

'Marshall. Look, here is my card. I am a senior civil servant at the Treasury although currently on extended leave. I am rich, in reasonable health, my interests include philately and the fine arts. I am looking for a woman to spend money on. The younger and more attractive she is, the better I shall be pleased. I have not the slightest intention of marrying such a paragon though I've no objection to your telling her that I have. So far as I know, I suffer from no social diseases. I have here twenty fifty-pound notes. I am about to tear them in half. Thus. I shall give you these halves, and keep these. They are no use to either of us unless paired off. You supply me with what I am looking for and you shall have my halves; if not you must return me yours. I think, Mrs Paget, that that covers everything, so I'll vacate your office in case you might wish to entertain Colonel Wagstaffe, or play bridge with a Majorcan duke.'

2

'*I* hear you're better.'

'Perhaps a little better, Jack.'

'You look better.'

'I look like fuck.'

'I never heard you swear before, Marshall.'

'Well, all of a sudden there seems no reason not to. How's my sister?'

'Fine, fine. A tower of strength.'

'Yes, she is, isn't she?'

'Sylvia sent her love. She couldn't make it this time, Marshall, because –'

'Oh come on, Jack, there's no need to lie to a dying man. I don't suppose she even knows you're here. Why are you here? Or should I guess?'

'You probably could. It's not difficult.'

'If the question is what I expect it to be then you can anticipate my answer.'

'We're talking investment here, Marshall. A guaranteed return of fifteen per cent – maybe twenty-five per cent net. These are the sorts of figures which could cause riots on the Stock Exchange floor.'

'They don't have a floor any more. Just screens.'

'I've done so much of the groundwork. I've got several of

the top restaurants lined up. It's just that boring old thing, cash flow.'

'No, Jack, no. Ask Sylvia.'

'You think I haven't? Just a kick-start, that's all. My God, I'd do it for you any day of the week.'

'I think you'd better go now, Jack.'

'I'll make you a director, a partner. Half-shares in everything, a going concern. All you have to do is sit back and watch the profits roll in. I've prepared some documents, a signature on the dotted line, a cheque, and I'll have the shares transferred this afternoon. Sylvia's already a director, so it would give your team a controlling interest. How about it, Marshall? Be a sport, eh?'

But Marshall had already closed his eyes. One of the few advantages of dying, he thought, was that people believed you when you pretended to be asleep. He tried to think of other advantages. Very soon he *was* asleep.

3

There had been fifty-three cartons in all. After he had opened the seventeenth, the money from the earliest cartons began to flow. Marshall wrote to Sir Archibald Munro, a formal letter in which he explained that he had lost all enthusiasm for the Treasury and he would be grateful if he could arrange for him to be released from his contract and sent whatever was due to him from the pension fund. After the twenty-third carton he spent the night with Michelle. After the thirty-first he had his interview with Mrs Paget, and a substantial cheque arrived with a letter from Archie.

Dear Marshall,

Your father was a great man. He would have seen your abandonment of your career at an unusually early age as a dereliction of duty. He was a great man because he put duty before self-interest. Maybe that is why he never made it to the top in the political arena. When we took you on you were one of the brightest young men of your year, of your generation even; now God knows what you are. A knighthood would have been yours, as you well know. I am writing to tell you that I have, not without reluctance, blocked it. You are a gifted, but selfish, man.

Despite the above I wish you well. We must each go to hell, I suppose, in our own way. That is something one comes to realise after a lifetime in the Civil Service.

Yours,
Munro

By now Marshall's loneliness was acute, and one February evening he took a taxi to a Park Lane hotel, where he sat in the bar with an absurd drink in front of him. The waiters were dressed in tight hipsters and colourful shirts, with cummerbunds around their middles and bandanas around their heads. They had evidently been trained to emulate the mateyness of South Pacific beach-combers, but their dead eyes betrayed them. They displayed all the mateyness of beached sharks. A series of localised wars, hijackings and bomb scares had had its effect upon the tourist trade (never at its heartiest in February), and Marshall estimated that waiters outnumbered punters by a factor of two.

A tall, elegant and well-dressed woman slipped into the chair next to his which he had ensured was vacant for just such an eventuality. She put her hand gently on his arm, and asked:

'Were you waiting for someone?'

'Possibly for you,' said Marshall, relieved to find that the stories he had heard of this bar in this hotel were accurate. He looked more closely at his companion, who was certainly handsome, though so heavily made-up that it was impossible to guess her age.

'How gallant of you to say so.'

'May I buy you a drink?'

'I can't think of a single reason why you shouldn't.'

The voice was hard to identify. Just as the cosmetics concealed the face, so the mid-Atlantic twang overlaid and smothered whatever was regional in the voice. However, Marshall thought, it's not the voice I shall be paying for, and he called over a waiter, who walked with such a rolling, piratical swagger that he might have been playing in the chorus of a Gilbert and Sullivan operetta. As the waiter took the order he winked, assuming a complicity which Marshall found detestable. For a moment he questioned what he was doing in such a place, ordering such a drink for such a companion, but he shut his mind to all such doubts, saying to himself: I am here to have a good time, as a man in the dentist's waiting room might mutter: 'I am here to ease the ache.'

Marshall considered various conversational options. 'Are you up in town for a day's shopping?', 'Where are you from originally?' and 'Lousy weather' were all dismissed as too banal. Eventually he settled on the non-committal:

'Unusual place, this.' His companion agreed that it was. 'I mean, not really like the South Seas at all.'

'Why, have you visited them?'

'No, but I've seen the movies.'

'You think they more accurately represent island life, do you?'

Marshall, half smiling, glanced into the woman's face to see if there was any hint of sarcasm, but the expression was politely blank.

'Really, I've no idea. I just thought that you know, London . . . February . . .'

'Well, I can't argue with any of that obviously,' said the woman, who then introduced herself as Corinne.

'Unusual name. Mine's Marshall.'

'You have a Plan?' inquired the woman, but again gave no indication that she was not entirely serious.

When the drinks arrived, Marshall noticed that he was served before Corinne.

4

'How would you like to get out of bed for a bit?' asked the suave Arab doctor.

'I should like that very much if you think that I am up to it.'

'Sitting in a chair isn't going to kill you. Staying in bed for too long is more dangerous. If you find yourself breathless, Mr Marshall, there is a face-mask in the wall, and all you need to do is place it over your face like so, and breathe normally. Your condition is not entirely stable, but it is certainly better than it was when I examined you last week. Have your housekeeper bring you in a dressing gown, unless you would prefer to use one of ours.'

Along with the silk Paisley gown, Jane brought a new batch of letters, most of them bills, or offers to purchase hideous and overpriced knick-knacks. But one was postmarked Tórshavn, Føroyar, and was addressed in a child's hand. Marshall opened it with the silver dagger awarded to him when he had displayed his Commonwealth first issues at a Royal Philatelic Society exhibition. So great was the interest in his stamps and so frequent and impertinent the invitations, requests and salutations which followed that he was never again to put his collection, or any part of it, on display.

Dear Mr Marshall,

You advertised last year for the first issues of our islands'
stamps, and these I have from my uncle, Jakob. He tells me
that they are worth much money, especially the surcharged
stamps, produced when your fine country occupied and
administered us in 1940 to keep away the Germans.

Now it is my wish to come and attend college in England,
and for this I need much money, so perhaps we can make a
good arrangement.

> Your faithful servant,
> E. Davidsen

Also: I have the stamp without the bar, and also the one
with the double surcharge, which I believe is good. They
are cancelled nice and gently from Hvalvik. But unused I do
not have any one of the three, nor do I believe that you will
find these, for no one I speak to has ever seen these, and the
post officer in Tórshavn says that all were sold only for
postage.

Marshall could scarcely believe it. After so long, after so
much trouble, to fall into his lap! The Danish Realm issues
were of no interest to him, having been produced in 1975, long
after his dateline, but the overprints, should they be genuine –
and Marshall had never heard of forgeries of this set (hard to
achieve, one would have to handle both the surcharge and the
cancellation) – would leave him wanting only Mauritius.

'Good news?' Jane asked. 'You look like the cat that got the
cream.'

'I hardly think that I do, but the news is good. The Faroe
Islands surcharges! Jane, I'm almost there. I must write at
once.'

But as he stretched out his arm for paper and pen, he gasped
for breath. Jane, carefully briefed by Dr Zilkha, seized the

face-mask and placed it over Marshall's nose and chin.

'Faroe Islands, huh! If I wasn't here to look after you, you wouldn't live long enough to see your blessed bits of paper.'

5

Corinne ate heartily. Marshall had taken her to the hotel restaurant, which was gloomily anonymous. There he felt more secure than his rash adventure warranted. Corinne's conversation startled Marshall. She had a quick smile and a pert answer to every question he asked. But her responses seemed mechanical, almost computer-generated. Not until Marshall asked for her opinion did the conversation die. She was, up to a point, curious about him too. When she asked him where he worked, and he told her about the Treasury, omitting only to add that he had left the place, he would happily have continued with a minor indiscretion or two, but she anticipated him:

'That must be very secret work, so I'd better not ask you any more about it.'

But what did he want from her? And why did he have this desire to pass the secrets of the Civil Service to a hooker? He started to explain about how the unemployment figures were doctored, about how Third World aid was not aid at all, and about the absurdity of money supply and inflation statistics and the ways in which documents were 'improved', and the techniques by which the improved documents were 'leaked', and the processes by which the improved, leaked documents were used to create a world of impressive and profound obfuscation. She watched him with amusement, and listened to him sporadically. The less response Marshall received the more indiscreet he became. He told her about ministers' peccadilloes, until he mentioned the most colourful peccadillo of the least colourful minister, whereupon she startled him by admitting: 'I was there.'

Of course she was a professional like him. He had almost forgotten that.

Did he want a relationship with the girl at all? Not really, no. In place of such dangerous speculation and encouraged by the gentle pressure of her thigh against his, he attempted to imagine her naked in the bed beside him. He failed.

Over coffee she seemed to grow impatient with the courtesies, and asked:

'Your place or mine?'

Her place was unexpectedly tasteful. If Marshall had been required to guess what he thought he might find, he would probably have opted for beaded tablecloths, lurid art-deco table-lamps and garish crochet-work on the settee. But Corinne's tastes ran more to Habitat than Liberty. She was too young for the nostalgia business; no gilt-framed Pears Soap poster reproductions here; her furniture looked as though it had arrived in kit form. The place was as tidy as a show-flat, and as well-maintained. She ushered him into the bedroom.

'This may be difficult,' Marshall said.

'I don't see why.'

'You may have surmised that I'm not used to this sort of a relationship –'

'You don't kiss on the first date?'

'And, if I'm embarrassed and gauche, you will make allowances.'

'Embarrassed *and* gauche? – how sweet! While on the subject of allowances, two hundred is usual for a full night. At least, darling, that is the minimum, you understand. Just put the money on the dressing table next to David Essex as Che

Guevara, and we need never refer to it again. Such a depressing topic. And now, why don't you just lie back on the bed, and let me do all the work. I'm sure that in the circumstances that would be quite the best. Gauche? What a welcome relief!'

Marshall obeyed. He shut his eyes and imagined himself lying on a beach under an orange parasol. It was not long before he felt Corinne's hand unbuttoning and unzipping him, and then Corinne's breasts brushing against his chest. As she removed the last items of clothing she turned her back to him. He pressed himself to her and putting his hand between her legs found himself fondling the traditional accoutrements of a man.

'Balls like gooseberries!' said Corinne. 'Can you believe your luck?'

6

The night after Jack's visit the terrors began. Marshall lay in his darkened room and a faint hum of electricity and muffled sounds from the street kept the silence from being total. The absolute silence of death – that was one aspect he had not considered. Darkness too. From where he lay there was a pale rectangle of light which was the curtained windows, just enough light to outline the furniture, the dishearteningly tasteful pictures on the walls, the foot of the bed. There would be neither light nor sound, and without light and sound what was there? Suppose that the soul did not leave the body, but stayed for an eternity, an infinitesimally slow deterioration in darkness, in silence. Which would be worse, the lack of any stimulus, or the total loss of personality, the absorption into . . . what? You might call such musings morbid, if you had much of your life ahead of you, but it was scarcely morbid to be anticipating what would come, what must come, the next day, the next week, the next month.

Marshall tried an old trick, an alembic which had worked in the past when the terrors had threatened to overwhelm him. One by one he opened his albums. The first began with Aden. Abu Dhabi was disqualified, having issued its tiresome stamps in 1964. Abyssinia came into the African section, but was filed under Ethiopia, a more attractive and persuasive name entirely. But Aden began the British Asia section with an attractively coloured and pleasantly straightforward set – the 1937 Dhows with Multiple Script CA sideways watermark. It had been a question as to whether the Bombay Postal Circle issues should feature here or under India, but the stamps had been printed in India, so that was decisive. Hence the album began with the dhows sailing peacefully in the harbour, greens and sepia and scarlet, blues and purples and carmine, browns and yellows. But the scene was not altogether peaceful. The dhows were flanked with scimitars, for one should take nothing for granted in that part of the world. The set, quite a valuable one, had formed part of the original carton, and Marshall had only had to replace the three-anna mint, which had a tear, scarcely noticeable unless you knew it was there, but then, of course, when you looked at it, you could see only the tear. Aden was followed by the States, Seijun and the Qu'aiti State in Hadhramaut, uninteresting stamps these, featuring tourist views and smug sultans.

And then, in his beleaguered mind, Marshall flipped the pages to the 1862 Antigua issues, the Corbould designs of the young Queen in profile, the real thing. SG1 was the joker. Was it blue-green without the watermark or green, yellow-green, or dark-green with the watermark? The rough perforations were the same in every case, fourteen to sixteen. Fortunately the Morley-Bright Detector had revealed beyond question that he had the right examples, mint and used without watermark and very fine.

He saw with brilliant clarity in his mind the Antiguan issues, the four sixpenny issues, all blue-green, perfect in their familiarity, perfect in their relationship one with another, perfect in what distinguished them, each from the other. He turned the imaginary page, and there they were again, the quadruplets lying together with their neat cancellations, all from St Johns, August, September, October and November 1862, pure chance which had produced that delightful symmetry. Blue-green, incorruptible.

As he mentally surveyed them and delighted in them, he slowly lost consciousness, the terrors erased from his mind.

7

Agnes and Jeremy, Sylvia's children, came to visit. Marshall was heavily sedated and unsure who these gaudy young people were. Agnes, the elder and taller and blonder, carried a paper bag. Jeremy, darker, muscular, more compact, carried a cardboard box. Jane stood up as they came in, her face creased with smiles. She too had been dozing, her dreams pastoral and filled with scudding clouds.

'Do you know who's come to see us? It's your nephew and niece. Isn't that sweet of them?'

Marshall tried to make sense of these words. He plucked 'nephew' and 'niece' out of the air, and, as soon as he could interpret these, the others fell into place around them.

'I brought you some fruit,' said Agnes, her voice doubtful. 'They're not grapes anyway. We passed a stall by the station and, bearing in mind what Jeremy had got you, well . . .'

She emptied her bag into the bowl of fruit, and the gooseberries lay there insidiously. They were swollen, purple and green, and the seeds were bursting through the skins.

'It's smart here. Mum had said, but all the same.'

'Aren't you going to take your coats off, children?' said Jane, bustling about them, secure in the role which she had played so confidently for the best part of a century. 'Then I'll organise a cup of tea for us all, shall I?'

Jeremy's present, once decanted, turned out to be a bonsai tree. Marshall, who had heaved himself up amidst a plethora of pillows, focused his eyes on something twisted and wrinkled and unusually sinister. Agnes announced that she found it incredibly ugly, but Jeremy insisted that it was the only thing to give a sick uncle.

'They're very old and Japanese,' he said. 'The woman in the shop said this one was especially old.'

'But not especially Japanese,' muttered Agnes.

'It's amazing,' said Marshall, and took a sip of orange juice to sweeten his mouth. 'And the gooseberries are too. I could tell you a story about gooseberries, but I won't.'

'He's not well,' said Jane at the door, 'he's rambling. A pot of tea will do us all good.'

Once she was out of the room Jeremy sat on the bed.

'You don't look so terrible,' he said.

'Pass muster, do I?'

'You pass the mustard very adequately.'

'For a dying man.'

Agnes asked: 'Are you really? Or should we talk about the weather?'

'Yes, really.'

'And are you scared?'

Jeremy seemed scandalised. 'Agnes! This is a no-go area.'

Marshall smiled wryly. 'There are no no-go areas. That doesn't sound quite as it should. And yes, I'm scared out of my wits. But it helps to talk about it.'

'See!'

'Agnes is considering giving herself to Christ. But why give when you can sell?'

'I'm also studying psychology,' said Agnes, with a mixture of pride and embarrassment. 'But if I do, I shall say a Mass for you, Uncle Marshall.'

'I'll look forward to that.'

'What's it *really* like though?' asked Jeremy. 'Being on the brink.'

Marshall chose his words with care. He spoke in short sentences these days, which was safer.

'If I look forward it's darkness. If I look back it's regrets. So I try and do neither. My stamps help. And maybe a gooseberry will.' Jeremy proferred the bowl and Marshall took a gooseberry, whiskery and rough, then sweet and sour, into his mouth. 'Yes, it does.'

Agnes took one too. 'Do you hope you'll have a remission? It does happen. The father of a friend of mine who had already had the last rites . . .'

'Of course I hope for a remission. I always wanted to be immortal. But it would be nice to rest.'

8

It seemed to Marshall that his room, his visitors, the doctor and the nurses were removing themselves, though with painfully deliberate slowness, from him. It was as though he were swimming out to sea and each time he turned to look at the shore and those disporting themselves on the beach, they were smaller and their voices fainter. But as they etiolated, so the image of his mother became more vivid. He remembered with great particularity one occasion when a banquet was being celebrated at Tall Trees. He knelt at the window and saw the Chinese lanterns swaying from the branches, mysterious pools of coloured lights and the shiny bonnets of the limousines reflecting and diffusing the porch lights, and the chauffeurs sharing a fag or two and a whiff of gossip. Snatches of their conversation would curl up to his dormer window, and bursts of laughter. When he grew cold or cramped he would slip back into bed.

His mother had pushed open the door of his room – she left it ajar so that she would be able to come in without waking him – and sat on the edge of the bed. She was wearing a black lace shawl around her shoulders – he thought of cobwebs against a white rock – and ruby earrings.

'Are you awake, darling?' she whispered. Her scent was the essence of *her* in his young nostrils. No one else could or ever should wear it. They must not! He feigned sleep. He thought he could see her through narrowed eyes without her noticing, but –

'So you are awake!' And she put her hand under the cellular green blanket and tickled his tummy. He wriggled and chuckled in delight. 'I've brought you a little something, un soupçon, une bonne bouche.' Whenever she spoke French to him it meant a treat. 'Open your mouth and shut your eyes!' It was a large chocolate with ribbed edges. Then without warning it exploded in his mouth, and a dribble of rum coursed down his chin. 'I shouldn't really,' she added. 'Goodness knows what your father would say.' The sickly sweet juice warmed and delighted him.

'Come in with me for a cuddle!' he said.

'I'll wrinkle my dress,' she said. 'It's silk and it creases.'

'Please.'

'I'd better take it off.'

She hooked two straps over her shoulders and stepped out of it. That easy! Within a moment, warm and soft, she was cuddling up to him, and the scent was everywhere. He burrowed into her.

'Wicked thing!' she murmured in delight, and licked the rum from his chin. A deep voice called out from the foot of the stairs. 'Oh lord,' she said, 'that means trouble. He'll be on the rampage now.'

Drawing her lips down his bony chest, she kissed his belly button, then rolled out of bed, covered him over, right over, with both the blanket and the quilted eiderdown, and by the time he could extricate his head she was gone.

9

When the Faroe Islands overprints arrived, Marshall examined them critically, found nothing to disturb him, and delicately inserted them into the Scandinavia album. Now he had twenty-nine albums completed, and was missing only Mauritius. He was not so out of touch with reality as to suppose that he would find these mint, since only two examples of the penny, and four of the twopence, were known to have survived, while fifteen and twelve respectively of the used stamps had. A single page would do. What had happened to these twenty-seven? There was one man who could tell him.

Harry Nissen had sat next to him at an auction when Marshall was disposing of stamps which were surplus to requirements, and Harry had bought one of Marshall's lots.

'Yours?' he asked. He was a small red-faced man who resembled a jockey or a farmer rather than a pasty-faced philatelist. He wore a black beret, which confused some people, because he was a Glaswegian Jew.

'How did you know?'

'Well, d'you see, when you leave your catalogue open like that, you're scattering clues like confetti. You'd marked the lot, yet didna bid for it; what conclusion should I draw? And did I do well?'

Having established that Harry Nissen was interested in buying what he had to sell, Marshall invited him round to the apartment and gave him tea and scones. Harry ate some scones and bought some stamps and invited him to be his guest at the annual dinner of the Philatelic Research Society.

'There will be a display by society members, but you'll not want to waste your time with that. Come in time for a wee dram before the dinner, and you'll be doing yourself a service, laddie. I told them if they wanted me as their President I would make the one condition. Only the twelve-year-old malt to be served. They agreed.'

There was little to be known about malt whisky which Harry Nissen did not know, and he knew more about the history of stamps than he knew about malt whisky.

'What I like,' said Harry, 'is the history, not the aesthetics, not the chemistry. Just who made them, when, why, where and how.'

The dinner was a disgrace, always was, according to Harry, and always would be, so long as they tried to do things on the cheap. 'The Treasurer runs his arsehole of a hotel, and he thinks that holding the dinner here will bring him new trade. Never has and never will. Who wants to eat bad food merely because it's cheap? His wife does the cooking. Stamp collectors may be anal, but they've got to put something in the other end too.'

There were toasts. To the Guests. To the President. To the Queen. To the Postmaster General. To Research. To the Society. To the Cook. To Absent Friends ('Lucky buggers!' Harry muttered in Marshall's ear). Each toast was drunk in twelve-year-old malt whisky. There was an auction. Since the assembled philatelists were a mean-minded bunch it was a low-key affair. Most of the lots were estimated by the vendors at considerably more than the purchasers were prepared to pay, so few changed hands. Harry, who conducted the auction, was not the most passionate advocate of what he was supposed to sell.

'You've all seen Martin's Middle Eastern rubbish on numerous occasions. I'm not surprised he's decided to sell it. As a collection of dubious and undesirable items, it is almost unique in philatelic history. But we have a totally unrealistic reserve of a fiver, so I suppose we'd better start at five, and, as your President, I will charitably start the bidding there, but for God's sake, somebody else bid, or I shall be left with the garbage.'

By the time the songs started, Marshall was enjoying himself.

So now Marshall asked Amelia Kellogg for a telephone to be brought to his bedside.

'Harry? It's Marshall. Good to find you in.'

'These sodding answering machines, I won't have them in the house. And they have the nerve to play Mozart at you! Mozart! The greatest genius this bastard world has ever seen and they use the poor bugger's music to keep you waiting on the telephone. But how are you, Marshall? I heard you were not so clever.'

'Not so clever at all, Harry. I could be seeing Mozart in person before too long. Shall I give him your felicitations?'

'Please. I have a letter of his to his dad, you know. An entire. Quite rude. They say that his rudeness is all down to some disease that makes you fidget and talk dirty. God help us all. You can't even be dirty any more without them putting a name to it and spoiling the fun. Sometimes, Marshall, I think I've had enough of it all. Could be I'll be joining you in the Arcadian fields. Suicide would be an option, except the bastards would go and put it all down to some medical condition. Would you like a bottle of something a bit special? Worth getting better for, I'd have thought. I'll send you one anyway. What the hell!'

'What I'm after, Harry, is the Mauritius Post Office penny and twopence.'

'Well of course you are, laddie. Who isn't?'

'Harry, it's complete. My first issue collection. Marcel got me the Portugal and then the Faroe Islands turned up out of the blue. Everything except Mauritius. Where would I find them?'

'I'll tell you what I have got. The penny orange-vermilion on yellowish paper, earliest impression, unused, ex-Ferran and Tomasini. Paid ten grand for it at the Gibbons Rarities of the World sale in '78. Would that help you, Marshall, eh?'

'No, Harry. It's the 1847 pair I'm after. I'd settle for used.'

'You'll bloody have to, and count yourself uniquely privileged if you do. Tomasini had them, of course, because he bought them from Ferran. Dale Lazar had some, I'm sure, and Caspar. But who's got them now? You don't feel like chatting up Her Majesty, I suppose? Now that she has to pay taxes, she might be short of a few readies, and I don't suppose they're much more than scrap paper to her.'

'There must be some left in private hands.'

'Could you pay?'

'Everything I've got, though it may not be enough.'

'Hmm. No heirs, eh? Nor me neither. Thought I had a love-child. Turned out to belong to the husband. Deeply disappointed. All those impressive stains on the sheets, counts for sod-all in the end, doesn't it? Well, leave it with me, laddie. No promises, mind, but I'll put out the odd feeler. Bit urgent I expect, eh?'

'Bit.'

'Do what I can. Mozart, eh? Ask him what he *really* thought of Da Ponte, eh?'

10

Marshall is overcome with weariness. Although the doctor, the nurses and Jane all pester him to sit for a while in the chair, to listen to music, to watch some rubbish on television – quelle horreur! – which they believe might edify, or at least divert, him, he refuses to move a muscle. In part, the reason is that his muscles sing out not to be moved; they are as tired as he is.

'I'll rest,' he says, 'and maybe tomorrow . . .' He notices them glancing at each other and knows what lies unspoken between them. Is this it? Will he ever leave his bed again? He wants to reassure them, tell them it's only the ache in the muscles, but he's too tired to speak to them. One of the nurses nursing his father had said: 'When the time comes, they're pleased to go. I've sat with scores of them, poor dears. It's always the same, they welcome it.' If what she claimed were true, then there was no cause to worry, for Marshall would not be pleased to go. No sir, no way, not yet.

He dreamt feverishly of Sylvia, when she was tiny, three or four, and he had been told to look after her on the beach. Although he had resented the charge because he had looked forward to climbing up the cliffs – some friends had challenged him to try the overhang – he had taken the duties seriously and had never let her out of his sight. But in his dream he buried her, and although she yelled out that the sand was burning, he continued to shovel the scalding coral-white sand on to her face, her eyes, her mouth. When she was quite covered, he lay on top of the place to cover the tell-tale signs of his activity. He could feel the sand shifting slightly under him, but pressed down with all his weight. Soon all movement ceased, and the sea swept in and covered them both, and that was as hot as the sand.

Sylvia was by his side when, covered in sweat, terrified, and unable to remember who or where he was, he awoke.

'The way you've been sleeping,' said Sylvia, 'no wonder you could never find a woman to marry you. It would have been like sleeping next to an army of Muslim insurgents.'

'I was having bad dreams. I dreamt –'

'Don't tell me. I have quite enough trouble coping with my own dreams. Dreams are extremely boring and nothing at all to do with anyone else.'

'I know that,' said Marshall, smelling his sweat and wishing he could have a bath and clean sheets – oh, and good health again, why not, he was not an old man after all. 'That's why dreams are so terrifying. Would you fetch me a nurse, Sylvia? I'm desperate to get out of these rags.'

'Well, yes I will, Marshall, in a moment, but there's something rather more important than personal hygiene which we ought to discuss. Jack came to see you and asked you to bail him out.'

'Listen,' said Marshall wearily, 'I lent you money, you were very grateful, and that was not long ago.'

'A month. Six weeks, actually.'

'I lose all sense of passing time in this place. But there you are. Six weeks. Well for Christ's sake, Sylvia, what happened to it? And didn't you have two cheques, one postdated?'

'It was generous of you, and the money went on Agnes's and Jeremy's school fees, and on getting the mortgage arrears out of the way; then there was this business of Jack's company collapsing.'

'I don't see how it could collapse. It was never really up and running, was it?'

'Marshall, you diddled me. Over the business of Father's will.'

Marshall pressed a bell on the end of a cable. The clinic was so over-staffed that the nurses seemed grateful to be summoned, and could be counted upon to arrive instantly.

'Sylvia, we've been through all this. He left all his money to you, and you had it. How you've managed to get through it all is the mystery. Sylvia, if it had not been for Jack . . .'

'Marshall, those boxes did not belong to you, because they did not belong to Daddy.'

'Not that old thing again . . .'

'Yes, Marshall. I knew all along. He told me. About Auerbach and about the others. Word got around, of course. Daddy asked me what I thought he should do about it. He was dying. I said to do nothing. He had told me and felt better for it.'

'Why didn't *you* tell *me*?'

'It was a stressful time, wasn't it? And after he died I just wanted it all to be finished. But things never are, are they? Not for the survivors. And now, instead of facing up to things, you're dying. Oh Marshall –' she pressed his hand – 'you're a holy terror and I don't know what I'm going to do with you.'

11

*I*t was the night before the wedding. Marshall arrived at Sylvia's Clapham flat and announced that he was taking her to dinner. Sylvia told him he was being absurd. Did he not appreciate what was involved in getting married? Men . . . Jesus! The flat was full of women Marshall had never seen before and to whom he was not introduced. The Praetorian Guard.

'What are they all doing, for crying out loud?' he asked.

'Helping. Women's things.'

'Can't they get on without you for an hour or so? Isn't that what helping means?'

Sylvia said that they could not, but the Praetorian Guard announced that it could. 'It'll do you good, take you out of yourself,' it mysteriously added.

'Who do they think I am?' asked Marshall. 'An ex-boyfriend?'

'They know all about you. They think the world of you. They were intrigued to learn that you're still a bachelor. Martine especially.'

'Yes, well . . .' Marshall muttered, as they entered a wine bar, staffed by Antipodeans dressed more appropriately for Bondi Beach than Clapham.

What Marshall had intended was to talk Sylvia out of

marrying Jack. He certainly tried. He asked his sister all the right questions and received all the wrong answers. Sylvia admitted that Jack was no dream-boat. When Marshall accused him of being a wastrel, Sylvia agreed that he was a bit irresponsible. When Marshall suggested that he was marrying Sylvia for her money, Sylvia simpered a little, but refused to deny it, adding: 'Other things too.'

'If he does you any mischief . . .'

'I'm sure that he will. But I'm a good deal more resilient, Marshall, than you suppose. And I can look after myself these days. Which isn't to say I'm not touched by your concern. But look at it this way. If you announced your engagement to a girl I didn't approve of, and I tried to talk you out of it, how would you react?'

Although like most snobs Marshall had never regarded himself as a snob, it was the vulgarity of the wedding which offended him. He was depressed by the unpleasant Victorian church with its missionary leaflets and exhibition of tribal arts and crafts, he was bored by the zealous ministrations of the priest whose forehead gleamed with self-abasement, he was irritated by the staff at the local hotel who handed out sausage rolls with the cheeriness of home-helps. Apart from Jack, his sister and the Praetorian Guard, he had no recollection of having met any of the guests before, and he wondered how on earth Sylvia had acquired such a mediocre bunch of acquaintances. Although clearly the star of the show, Marshall was more embarrassed than gratified by the attentions he received. He was outraged that it fell to him to give his sister away to so unworthy a groom.

Telegrams were read out by the best man, a tow-headed wreck who promoted records for an American music company. He made several jokes involving singers and musicians, whose names meant nothing to Marshall. Then it was Marshall's turn to speak.

The master of ceremonies, a bucolic market-gardener

whose heartiness was thought to qualify him for this lucrative sideline, announced him as 'the influential son of an internationally famous father, one who helped to make this good old country of ours great'.

Marshall emptied his glass of substitute champagne, and gazed despondently at his flushed sister and her hideous friends.

'It is customary on such occasions to make jokes, and to tell unsavoury stories about the bride's early life. I shan't do that. There was nothing unsavoury about Sylvia, and she has never done anything to forfeit my love or respect, although by deciding to marry Jack she has stretched my tolerance close to its limit.' Anxious chuckles greeted this. It was a satirical remark, wasn't it? Ironic? If only the man had smiled when he said it. 'I wish the couple well, of course, and a long and happy life together.' Ah, that was better. 'But I have to say that if Jack proves to be unworthy of my sister, I shall see to it that he lives to rue the day. To Sylvia and Jack!'

The champagne went down and the bride and the Praetorian Guard removed themselves. Marshall was cornered by Jack between a potted palm and a mosaic representation of Civic Pride.

'You don't need to worry, you know,' said the unblushing groom. 'I do love her – after my fashion.'

'I thought marriages were made in heaven, not the bankruptcy courts,' said Marshall, who had been doing some research.

'That's a bit below the belt, old man. I'm a reformed character now, and I couldn't be a reformed character if I hadn't had my ups and downs.'

'Tell me about the ups.'

'Secrets of the bedchamber.' Jack put a finger to his nose.

'I'm not an intolerant sort of person. I meet all sorts in my professional life. I'll give you the undeserved benefit of a very considerable doubt, Jack, but don't push me too far. If it's a case of who has my sister's interests closest to their heart, it's no contest. The situation calls for careful scrutiny and impeccable auditing. Where are you going for your honeymoon by the way?'

'Monte Carlo,' said Jack.

12

The redoubtable Amelia Kellogg arrived. A blanket bath from Amelia was about as comforting as being in drydock and having barnacles scraped off your hull. Nevertheless, in the circumstances it seemed preferable to an inquisition from Sylvia. Since Sylvia showed no signs of leaving, Amelia put screens around the bed. From time to time Marshall was confronted by the accusing face of his sister peering round the edge of the barricade.

'You've lost a lot of weight, Marshall,' she said. 'Which you badly needed to do. If you get shot of this lot, then you'll be a new man. All this pampering!' she added as Amelia turned him with something of the delicacy of a fireman shifting rubble. 'I had the money and you had the boxes, and the boxes were worth more than the money, but you never said.'

'It was a long time ago,' said Marshall, as Amelia scrubbed around his genitals, like a gardener pulling up carrots. 'And if you felt you had a grievance, you should have said so at the time. It's far too late now.'

'We shall go to the wall,' said Sylvia. 'Will you at least leave us something in your will?'

The following day Harry Nissen called.

'Interesting poser you set me with that Mauritius business. There's four pairs "off the market", one in the Royal

Collection, one at the BM, one in Berlin, and one in Stockholm. There seem to be three sets of the Mauritius first issue in private hands. Could be more, but I've only traced three. One belongs to an American called Vernon Gwatkin. Which is bad news for you. He made a pile out of Lycra, whatever that is, and is making another pile out of semolina. I think they said semolina. Is that possible? Point is, he's not short of a bob or two. He lives up a mountain in California, guarded by a herd of pit-bull terriers. In short, Vernon is no Little Mary Sunshine, and there's no way you're likely to get close enough to his stamps to have a sniff of them.

'An Australian politician called Humphreys has got a set, but he keeps them in the bank, and has apparently never shown them to a living soul. He has an especial detestation of the British, apparently, and he put the phone down when I rang him up to ask about the Mauritius. I don't think you have a wooden hoop in Hades' chance with him, frankly, laddie.

'Your best hope seems to lie with two unmarried sisters living in Wakefield. Susan and Martha Turnbull. They inherited a superb British Commonwealth collection – gold medals galore – from an uncle, and they have shown signs of disposing of some classic stamps in recent years. There was an article about them in *Philatelist Monthly*. You want I should contact them on your behalf?'

'What's the deal, Harry?'

There was a mellifluous chuckle on the line.

'Thought you might ask. Nothing up front, Marshall. I mean, between friends . . . But if I do get them for you, you bequeath them to me, right?'

Marshall was outraged. 'If I do that, the collection will no longer be complete.'

'If you don't, it will never be complete. This way you'll have them to enjoy. And you could outlive us all. I could give you five years, Marshall, did you know that? And I've got a liver which looks not unlike a traffic accident. So: if I get them, you have them. And I only get them back if you predecease me. I tell you, man, I'm too generous to live.'

'I'll think about it.'

'Let me at least negotiate for you. They may not want to sell them after all. Spinsters. Yorkshire stock. It's never going to be a doddle. If they agree, I'll come and get the cash off you. If not, what have you lost?'

13

Marshall could not bring himself, after the humiliations he had endured with Corinne, to undertake further romantic adventures. Better to be lonely than betrayed.

One day Celia Wasserman contacted him. Not business, she said, that was all sorted out now. Social. She was having a few friends for dinner, nothing formal, just some friendly gossip around a pot-au-feu, and would he care to join them? He said that he would have to shift a few appointments around and would get back to her. He conjured up her cool and challenging beauty. He remembered the delicacy of her wrists, the smallness of her ears, the agreeable scent which wafted from her. Images of Corinne intervened. Desire was replaced by anxiety. He never returned Celia's call. Latterly there were times when he hoped she would be more persistent, but the hammer had fallen. She was younger than he by a quarter of a century.

He turned instead to the pleasures of the inanimate. As the cartons were sifted through and disposed of from his storage flat, they were replaced by other boxes. These contained pornography by the sackful, magazines, photo-sets and video films, which he bought by mail.

He was as assiduous in collecting and sorting these as he was later to become with his stamps. He was after a certain type of beauty, and anything which approximated to that standard, he filed; anything else he dropped down the rubbish chute. There were complaints. The unctuous landlord's agent visited Marshall. The agent stooped and peered up at people.

'It appears that this exuberant material emanates from your flat, Mr Marshall. Now what have you to say to that?'

'I am not obliged to say anything.'

'But are you not ashamed, a man of your years?'

'Not at all. I am delighted that I remain sexually active, although I am unclear as to what business it is of yours. Are you jealous perhaps, Mr Hartigan? Do you have potency problems?'

The agent, who had lank, yellow hair like waterweed, beat a fist into the palm of his hand. But although there may have been a message in this gesture, he failed to clarify it further. Marshall showed him out, but after the agent's departure he noticed that his hands were shaking.

The beauties which he identified and hoarded were the strong athletic types. Active girls and women. The video he played most frequently depicted a tall woman playing a hectic tennis match against an older, fatter man. From time to time she bent to collect a ball and the camera lingered on her knickered bottom. Later, when the match was over and she had won, they sat on a bench to recover, and the man fondled her breasts, releasing them from the constraints of dress and brassière. She took him back to her flat, where, after some foreplay, he inserted first a tennis ball, then the handle of the racket, into her vagina, to her apparent (though improbable) delight. They were interrupted at this stage by the arrival of her flat-mate, a darker, more sultry type of girl who seemed initially shocked, then intrigued at what she was witnessing. The threesome that developed was athletic and inventive, but less interesting to Marshall than the preliminaries. It was the tennis game, and the promise of what it would lead to, that excited him. He loved to see the woman's sweat, and the fine blond hairs (for the film was of very reasonable quality) on her tanned arms and legs. He would freeze the frame on one of these scenes and bring himself delightedly to climax.

Weeks later, sorting some papers from the Tall Trees days, Marshall found a photograph of his mother and father on the tennis court. The moment captured by the photographer uncannily replicated one of the more innocent moments from the film.

14

As he had light-heartedly suggested, Harry Nissen was too innocent to live. He should not have mentioned the names of the Turnbull sisters, nor that they lived in Wakefield. It was not difficult for Marshall to make contact with them.

He spoke to Martha Turnbull on the telephone. Initially she was reserved and extremely suspicious. He explained who he was, and whose son he was, which produced the hoped-for impact on the sisters. But why, they were curious to know, was he telephoning them? He was a philatelist? Well, that was most interesting, as they too had a collection of which they were inordinately proud. Would he care to come and take tea with them, and have a look through it? He would indeed. The suggestion had come from them. How extremely accommodating! But when could he come, they wanted to know. He warned them that he was none too well just at the moment, but if he made a special effort, he was sure that he could make it up the M1 on the Tuesday following. Martha promised him that they would have everything ready against his arrival. But would he really be well enough to travel? He reassured them that it was just an enervating bug. Martha spoke of an old-fashioned tonic which they had always found a great comfort. They would take a bottle off the top shelf and have it ready. And a jar of Mexican honey, not that horrid blended stuff.

By Tuesday, Marshall had anticipated that Arthur Winepress would have the cash for him. He also expected some opposition from the hospital to his planned expedition, and he was right.

'It is quite impossible, this trip you have planned! I cannot believe that you seriously intend it.'

The brown-eyed doctor, usually so considerate and docile, with his treacle voice and his immaculate manners (a combination of Arab deference and public school charm), was crosser than Marshall had believed possible.

'I certainly do intend it, doctor, which is why I wanted you to come and discuss the arrangements with me.'

'It is not just possible, but probable, that it will kill you.'

'Why?'

'Why? Well, because you will be subjected to violent movement, to changes in temperature. You will have to be detached from the saline drip, you will be deprived of oxygen; it simply cannot be permitted.'

Marshall smiled encouragingly: 'When I was brought here, I came in an ambulance. As I recall, it was fitted out for every possible eventuality. And as to changes of temperature and violent movements, there simply weren't any. Then again, saline drips and oxygen masks are standard equipment on most of your ambulances, are they not?'

'But an ambulance is not a charabanc. We are not talking of pleasure cruises.'

'That is exactly what we are talking of, Dr Zilkha. You have ambulances. I wish to hire one for next Tuesday for my pleasure cruise. This clinic is a profit-making institution. You can hardly deny that, when you present me with bills more appropriate to Cipriani's or the Georges Cinq. Well then! I am offering you a substantial profit, and I do not see how you can justify refusing me. I can perfectly well turn to Yellow Pages and find another ambulance, although, since that is likely to be less well appointed, you would risk losing me, and the fees I pay (which I pay very promptly), sooner than if you play ball. Oh, and I'll need a driver, of course.'

This excellent speech had exhausted Marshall, and he scarcely had enough energy left to raise a smile, when Dr Zilkha ('against his better judgement', he added prudently) agreed. But Marshall would have to sign a document releasing the clinic from any responsibility for the possible consequences. He seemed to spend his life indemnifying people.

Predictably, Jane was furious. She took the party line and claimed he was signing his death warrant.

'Why you? Others can do it. I could do it, Marshall. You have no consideration for other people, never did have. That poor sister of yours. Why does she put up with it? Why do any of us? And now Mr Winepress tells me that you're about to blow most of what you've got left on this crazy scheme.'

And so on.

The only one who was at all sympathetic was Stacey Anne, whom Marshall invited to accompany him in the ambulance to Wakefield. He needed a qualified nurse, and anyone would be better than that Kellogg woman.

'Might,' said the Darlin' Girl from Clare. 'But no funny business. Keep well away from the knicker elastic. I've got other fish to fry.'

What she meant was that she had received an invitation from Marcel. He wanted her to work for him in Carcassonne. 'And we all know what that means!' added Stacey Anne delightedly. 'So I intend to remain faithful to him, until I see him again. That's the least I can do. Don't you think so? But I will help you out this once, Marshall, because all the others are so agin it and because if it hadn't been for you I wouldn't have met the old bugger at all. Did you know, by the way, that that's what Frenchmen like to do, along with the other things? I was really shocked. Dirty pigs! I wonder what on earth he'll think of next . . .'

Sex and food and stamps. As Marshall had become weaker he had lost interest in the first, as the others became more and more prominent in his mind. A cup of coffee, brought grudgingly to him by Amelia, tasted like no cup of coffee ever tasted before. He could almost distinguish each ground. He ordered more extensively from the elegant menu. The raspberries were astonishing. He ate them one at a time, one succulent, one overripe and tasting almost of blood, one sharp and pungent, one redolent of mould. He wished Agnes would bring more gooseberries. He had never before been aware of how many tastes there are in a slice of cucumber, the skin, the meat, the seeds, all quite distinct, or an apple or a loaf of bread.

Jane was encouraged: 'My, but you're eating heartily,' and set about arriving each day with tempting delicacies. Some of these were not a success. A box of liqueur chocolates, which he sampled with enthusiasm, made him feel queasy for several hours.

His sense of smell was also heightened. He had never really understood what people meant when they referred to the 'bouquet' of a wine. Now he did. It was like plunging your nose into a bunch of flowers. To drink the wine seemed an irrelevance.

He left the oxygen mask on the wall.

He got them to dismantle the drip.

'There'll be plenty of time to play with that toy,' he said, 'in due course. Just be patient.'

He could taste and smell the air around him.

On Monday, Arthur Winepress arrived with the money, and Harry Nissen called.

'I brought a million in cash,' said Arthur. 'My power of attorney was stretched to the limit, I can tell you. The bank looked at me as though I were some kind of master con-artist; with a good deal of respect, in other words.'

Arthur had brought the money in a large attaché case, 'like in the movies'. There were two hundred packets of bundles – a hundred per bundle – of fifty-pound notes. Was that a million pounds? As a child, Marshall had reckoned money in terms of the choc-bars he could buy with it, and imagined rows and rows of them in their garish silver wrappings, stretching almost to infinity. A briefcase of banknotes seemed insignificant compared to all those choc-bars. And he was preparing to swap the bundles for a few little slips of engraved paper. Judged by weight, the Mauritius stamps would be worth more than anything in the universe – except possibly the British Guiana stamps.

'There's not a lot left in the account,' Arthur warned. 'If anything happened to this lot, you could be living in Cardboard City.'

Harry arrived just as Arthur was leaving. A red-faced Scottish Jew and a florid country accountant sidled round each other like fighting cocks. After Arthur left Harry required to know who he was.

'My accountant.'

'Aye, I can believe it. He looks like he's been having a pint or two in the blood transfusion unit. I've got good news for you, son – I've got an appointment to see the Turnbull women. A suspicious pair of old biddies they are for sure. Seemed to regard yours truly as wholly untrustworthy. Didna tell them the whole truth though. They seem to think I'm a furniture restorer, and I thought it best not to disabuse them.'

Marshall was alarmed. Now that Harry had come up with the information, his usefulness was at an end.

'I've changed my mind, Harry.'

'What do you mean, man? You canna do that. The trouble I've taken on your behalf. You wouldna credit it.'

'I'm sorry, but it was what Arthur just told me. I haven't got the funds, Harry, indeed I haven't. Not for the Mauritius.'

'But you don't know how much they'll want yet, do you? Jesus wept, man, have you lost your senses since you've been in here? And speaking of which, what's this place costing you, for the love of the Lord?'

'Private Patients Plan.'

'Nah. They've not enough in their coffers to pay for this lot. Marshall, you've strung me along.'

Marshall was sitting in the chair beside the bed; his skin was grey and stretched tight over his chest. The pyjamas hung loose from his shoulders.

'Harry,' he said, 'I'm not feeling too great. I'm sorry you've had a wild-goose chase.' Gasping, he pulled the oxygen mask over his face and inhaled deeply. Although he was feigning, he felt easier almost at once.

'Aye, I'm sorry too,' Harry was saying, 'but not so much for meself. What's a phone call or two between friends? But it's the friendship itself I'm sorry for; I rather think that's dead already.' Then he added: 'Are you sure, man? We have little enough in this world without friendship.' Another pause. 'Is this how you want me to remember you, Marshall?'

Apparently it was.

When he was awakened on Tuesday morning, Marshall felt so weak that he was tempted to take the doctor's advice and call off the trip. Harry could have undertaken the commission. Harry might still be prepared to do it, if he, Marshall, were to make an abject telephone call. But could he trust Harry? He had not thought so before, and nothing had changed. Whom could he trust if not himself?

The arrangements proved unexpectedly straightforward. The orderly and Jane, who had taken to sitting up in his room all night, transferred him to a hospital trolley, and along with the first album (Aden to Baghdad) in his series he was rattled through the sparkling corridors to the waiting ambulance. He passed an old man in a dressing gown who looked pityingly (it seemed to Marshall) down into his eyes.

'I'm not dying,' Marshall muttered, 'I'm off to Wakefield.'

At the double doors leading into the real world, Marshall remembered that something vital was missing, and sent Jane back for the attaché case. He wondered if Arthur had told her what it contained. He thought probably not. Arthur had locked it and tied the key to his, Marshall's, watch strap, so that should be all right.

'I should like to ask you a number of questions while we have the opportunity,' said Stacey Anne, as they hummed along the M1 in the ambulance, which was, as Marshall had predicted, just as comfortable as his room in the clinic, and a good deal more private. 'We're not stupid in Ireland, you know, although we are denied a good many aids to learning. The nearest library to where I lived in Clare was more than a day's journey away, and the only literature we had in our house was the racing form. So I need you to educate me a little before I go to Carcassonne and Marcel. He's read books, do you see, and quite long ones too, and I don't want him treating me like an eejit.'

Jane, sitting at Marshall's feet, looked sourly at her rival, who enjoyed a superior position.

'Now you're not to tire him, Stacey Anne, with your stupid questions.'

'The first one isn't stupid,' Stacey Anne insisted, bridling. 'It's about Andrea Dworkin, whom I was reading about in the newspaper, where she said that women didn't enjoy sex. Is that true, do you think, Marshall? And if it isn't, why did she say it?'

'Of course it's true, stupid girl!' Jane snapped.

Marshall muttered: 'It may be true. I sometimes wonder if men do.'

'Everyone says that they do,' Stacey Anne continued, 'but then they would say that, wouldn't they, if they thought that other people did, because they wouldn't want to be the odd ones out. That's if they didn't. But if they did, I can't think of any reason why they'd say they didn't. They always seem to enjoy it in the movies. That Jeremy Irons, for instance. You see, it wasn't something we could ask the nuns. Right. Next question: should an innocent young girl believe what an older man says?'

Jane said: 'That's not a question to ask a man.'

'But if I ask *you*, I know what you'll say. You'll say, Of course not, so there's no point in asking you. But with Mr Marshall, I never know what he's going to say about anything.'

'If a man says what you want him to say, believe it,' said Marshall; 'if not, not. Not that it matters what he says, or what you believe.'

Stacey Anne's third question was the one that infuriated Jane.

'Are you afraid of dying?'

Marshall had no opportunity of answering that question, because the ambulance skidded to a halt. Jane caught the drip as the stand rocked dangerously. There were excited shouts from outside the vehicle and banging on the doors. These opened, and the ambulance driver's fresh face peered in. 'Major problem,' he said. 'There's been a pile-up. No way through.'

A middle-aged man in an anorak: 'Can you take my daughter to the hospital? She's cut about the face. Please. I'll make it worth your while. Please.'

The driver started to explain that he was not available for errands of mercy, when an anxious woman interrupted him.

'There's dozens of people hurt out here. Aren't you going to do something about it?'

Stacey Anne said: 'I'm a trained nurse. I'll see what I can do,' and jumped down from the ambulance. Marshall asked the driver whether he could find another route north.

'See for yourself, sir,' the young man said, and indicated that the road behind them was now a solid mass of traffic. 'There's no going forward and there's no going back.'

The middle-aged man, who had disappeared, reappeared with a ten-year-old girl in his arms. There were jagged cuts on her face, and blood was pouring from her right eye. The girl was whimpering.

'Do something for her,' he said, turning to Jane, whom he supposed to be more sympathetic than the men, 'you have to do something.' At which moment, Marshall began gasping for breath.

It was seven hours before they got Marshall back to the clinic, and they had not been within a hundred miles of Wakefield. Stacey Anne had stayed with the injured on the motorway. Marshall remembered nothing of the journey home. But as a porter was wheeling him along the corridor, with Jane holding his hand, he opened his eyes and stared at the housekeeper.

'Where's my attaché case?'

15

*T*here had been three periods of Marshall's life when he had been entirely happy. His early childhood at Tall Trees before his mother died, the time of his brief liaison with Jacqueline before she died, and the months when he had devoted himself to sorting, selecting and organising his collection of stamps.

Marshall had met Jacqueline during his first year as a civil servant. She had been his mentor, responsible for showing him the ropes, and she had shown him the ropes, cleats, halyards, rigging and all. Ten years his senior, she had endured a marriage which had ended after six tumultuous months. She showed Marshall photographs of the wedding. Eddie, her husband, wore flared trousers and a flowery tie. Jacqueline's family huddled around them. They looked to Marshall like a rugby team.

'You were the hooker?'

'To Eddie I was.'

'Why did you marry him?'

'To get away from home. And to be independent. Just shows how wrong you can be. I crawled back home within the year in a state of utter dependence. I could hardly make myself a cup of tea.'

Jacqueline had regained her freedom. 'Shouting, "I will no

longer be dictated to!" I went out and got myself a job as a secretary. I sometimes feel that a broken marriage is a prerequisite for female emancipation.'

Jacqueline was very beautiful. Everything about her was straight and long, her legs, her hair, her teeth, her nose, her fingernails. She wore little make-up at a time when most women wore a lot, and became something of a trendsetter (not difficult, she claimed) in the Statistical Department, to which she had been promoted. Women admired her, because, when they confided in her, she kept faith with them. Also because she dressed beautifully, more like a woman in a women's than in a men's magazine. Men were attracted to her but daunted. When they dared to ask her out, she put a friendly hand on their arm and apologised, merely saying: 'Thanks, but no,' or: 'Better not.' When it became apparent that she could manage without any of them, they called her frigid or a lesbian, but they were defining their own inadequacy. She was first to arrive in the morning, and often stayed late, covering for others who had dates or indispositions. She had a flat in Kensington which she kept immaculately tidy, and sometimes called in at Brompton Oratory on her way home. She prayed for love and companionship; and, if neither of them was to come her way, for strength to manage her life as it was. Her prayers, she realised, would be answered when she no longer needed to pray.

Marshall amused her. He was rich and well connected. He was tall enough and handsome enough, without the dangerous good looks that her husband had possessed. When she discovered that he was also sexually inexperienced, she was intrigued, as well as amused. He had been in the department a month when he remarked to her in the canteen:

'There must be more to it than this.' She thought he was speaking philosophically, but he was referring to the department. 'How can so many intelligent people spend their lives on something so trivial?'

'The government doesn't regard it as trivial.'

'They don't act on our advice.'

'Usually not, that's true. But it doesn't have to be trivial to be ignored.'

'And they doctor the figures in their public statements.'

'It would be remarkable if they didn't. In any case the figures we supply them with have already been doctored. How do you suppose we acquire the figures? If you have to supply your superiors with what you think they want or what they ought to have, which would you go for? What they actually require is expert advice to disregard. And experts to blame when the sums don't add up. The beauty of the British system is that Whitehall can always take the blame when Westminster gets it wrong. In return we have security of tenure and they don't.'

It was she who invited him out. A friend of hers was organising a charity concert, and was concerned that so few tickets had been sold. 'Bring somebody from work.' A couple of the secretaries were otherwise engaged, so she invited Marshall.

He could scarcely believe his luck. He was stunned by her beauty and impressed that she seemed so unconcerned about it. He was dazzled at how capable she was. Her car was always clean inside and out. Just as they say you should dance with someone before making love to them, so you should study their car and their driving before marrying them. Marshall hoped – except that it seemed too much to hope – to marry her.

The first time he visited her flat, he expected to find the bathroom cabinet crammed with creams and pills and aids to loveliness. He found Nivea cream.

She cooked him meals, and lent him books: Virginia Woolf, Iris Murdoch, Toni Morrison, Germaine Greer. He lay in bed with her and read chapters from his favourites, Waugh and Wodehouse. She took him to a Stanley Spencer exhibition and talked to him about composition and the Slade and the difficulty of achieving realistic flesh tones. How did she know about such things? He took her to a test match which was rained off. She knew a good deal about cricket too.

She saw little of him at work. Their offices were in different buildings and the game they played was to keep their office relationship as formal and proper as possible. Jacqueline spoke to him in the cheerfully anodyne voice she used for other male colleagues. Once, unobserved, sharing a crowded lift with him, she pressed her hand to his thigh.

She took the initiative also in their love-making. He would lie on the bed, under instruction not to move. She would undress him, anoint him with Nivea, caress him, excite him with her lips, climb on to him, and, as soon as he came close to climax, remove herself. They would make love for hours. The bedclothes would end up on the floor, so would they. He had known no pleasure to equal it, nor ever would again.

She enrolled him on a course of sexual instruction which taught him as much about himself as about her. One night he would have to name and touch every part of her body; another night she would hold him inside her but forbid him to reach a climax; another time he was required to bring home a large selection of representative sex aids and follow the instructions which came with each. Her body became familiar to him, but the more familiar it became, the more mysterious its functions. She taught him to cosset and respect his own body. He felt as though he was receiving instruction into some arcane religious order. He spent office hours anticipating the nights and carried her scent on his skin.

He pleaded with her to be allowed to move into her flat, or for her to move into his. She would not, could not, endure it. He explained that it was inconvenient and uneconomic to stay as they were. She agreed. When finally he admitted that, kept apart from her, he missed her dreadfully, and that it must mean that he loved her, she accepted that they would live together when details could be worked out. But they never did. Crossing the road to work, she was struck by a stolen Mercedes, and never regained consciousness.

It was an outrageous loss. He felt he had had his future stolen from him; there was no compensation. He had truly loved her.

What made his desolation almost too much to bear was that there was no one with whom he could discuss his loss. Nobody knew about it. Jacqueline's family – the rugby team – moved into action, and by the time the dust cleared there was no more Jacqueline. The funeral was private, and he never discovered when and where it was to take place. The body was cremated. The flat was locked up and put on the market. Marshall even considered buying it – surely something of her still lingered there – but was overcome with such emotional lassitude that for a while he was quite incapable of taking any decisions (apart from professional ones) at all.

Emotionally he never recovered from the loss. He was inconsolable and incomplete.

A while later, on a bank holiday, he visited Sylvia at a residential college where she was being taught a bewildering variety of subjects, including hotel management and – could he possibly have got this right? – macramé. They strolled in the sunshine along a riverbank cluttered with supermarket trolleys. She said that although it was a lovely surprise to see him, he seemed sad.

'It's like spending the afternoon with a civil servant,' she said wittily.

What stopped him from confiding in her was the memory of how he had interfered in her love life just a couple of years before. She could never have said serve you right to him because she never discovered how she had been betrayed. But the sympathy which she should have been bound to offer him would, in the circumstances, have been no comfort to him at all. He took her out to tea and returned her to the bleak college room which she had touchingly attempted to make more homely with family photographs, knick-knacks from her room at Tall Trees and a crocheted bedcover of indescribable hideousness. After a clumsy embrace and a peck of a kiss he left, leaving Sylvia bewildered, and himself more alone than ever.

16

As Marshall had grown sicker, it was not only the smell and taste of his food which had grown more vivid, but the colours of his dreams. Often he revisited the exhibition hall with the illuminated glass cases. Now there was only one empty – the one with the sign proclaiming Mauritius; the colours of those which were filled dazzled the senses. Venetian Red, Carmine, Magenta, Grey-Green, Turquoise Green, Dull Green and Emerald, Prussian Blue and Indigo, Lavender and Ultramarine, Slate Blue, Slate Violet and Slate Purple, Maroon and Mauve, Sepia and Chocolate, Ochre and Buff, Bistre and Lake and Drab.

'What colours are those?' he asked the curator, a huge man in a black surcoat, with black skin, and a salmon-coloured cravat.

'All colours known to man are here,' replied the curator, but his lips did not move, though the words reverberated in the empty hall, 'the others you may experience later.'

'We see through a glass darkly,' said Marshall.

'You understand well,' said the curator pompously. 'All is prepared for you. It will not be long.'

When Marshall awoke, Jane was by the bed, but although he was aware of a presence, he could not at first identify her.

'Who are you?' he cried out, but could not hear the answer.

'Where do dreams come from? From within or without?'

When he had fully recovered consciousness, he was unable to remember asking these questions, but Jane repeated them to him, and said that in her opinion dreams were to do with what you ate for supper, and that it was well known that cheese was the worst.

'You have visitors,' said Jane. 'That nice sister of yours and her husband.'

Marshall remembered then more than he cared to.

'Where's the attaché case?'

Jane patted his hand. 'Safe and sound, so you don't have to worry. It became detached when the ambulance driver jammed on his brakes. But there are still honest people in the world despite what the newspapers would have us believe.'

'I don't wish to see my nice sister,' he said, and his voice was so faint that Jane had to put her ear close to his mouth. 'But I'll see Jack, and you are to leave us alone.'

It was not easy explaining to Jack what he wanted of him. The words were clear in his mind, but ballooned in his throat and emerged from his mouth distorted. Marshall pointed at the oxygen mask, which Jack placed over his mouth, after which things were easier.

'The Turnbull sisters have got the stamps, Jack. I've got the money.'

'Are they willing to sell?'

'Probably.'

'And if so for how much?'

'Whatever it takes. The less you pay for them, the more you keep for yourself.'

'And if they won't sell, Marshall?'

'I want the stamps.'

Jack stood up, crossed to the window, stared out. His blazer was worn, though the buttons had been polished. The shoes were astonishing, but he looked like a man who had not come through.

'You've been in touch with them?' he asked.

'I had an appointment to see them. I never made it.'

'Would they recognise you?'

'They heard my voice.'

'So in the event of anything happening, your name would crop up?'

'I suppose so. Yes.'

'But you have a perfect alibi. You being confined here, Marshall, and them being wherever they are.'

'Wakefield.'

'Precisely.'

'I do, yes, depending upon the discretion of others.'

Marshall tried to heave himself into a more upright position, but, emaciated as he had become, there was no strength in his arms. Jack had moved beyond the range of his vision.

Jack said: 'It doesn't sound like too much of a problem.'

'From where I lie,' muttered Marshall, 'it is a problem.'

'You want something and you have money to buy it with. They have something to sell and probably need the money. That is the sort of problem which is right up my street.'

'Glad to hear it.'

His mouth tasted of decay, and the words were like dried peas. Haltingly Marshall explained his reluctance to give so much cash to his brother-in-law. Jack appeared incredulous.

'You don't trust me? I may have my shortcomings but I'm not that desperate. I'll take Sylvia with me if you like.'

But Marshall did not like. His sister was to be kept out of it. The problem remained. Would Jack betray a dying man? Would he take the money and run? Would he abscond and turn up on a Brazilian beach and abandon Sylvia? It all seemed alarmingly probable.

'How will I recognise the stamps, old boy? If they've got so many . . .'

'I only want two. I've got some facsimiles, poor copies, but

179

they'll aid identification. Early Mauritius, you see, are numerous. It was the first British possession to issue stamps. The penny one is orange-red, and the twopenny deep blue. In imitation of the mother country, you see. And this is the important thing. The first set has the words "Post Office" running up the left side. All the others say "Post Paid". They were engraved on copper by the local watchmaker and jeweller in Port Louis, and he made the plate on the reverse of an advertisement for a local hotel. His name was Joseph Barnard; he did a good job, Jack.'

'So will I.'

Marshall was exhausted. His eyes were like jewels in putty. He muttered: 'Your children came to see me, Jack. I liked them.'

Amelia Kellogg interrupted them and set up the drip for the night. Jack stayed while she did so. Outside in the lobby, Sylvia was waiting. Her voice would be honeyed, but her eyes full of recrimination. When Jack arrived home, there would be messages he had no wish to deal with, and bills he could not pay. He would tell Sylvia that Marshall had work for him, but not the details. As soon as he could get the money out of Marshall, he would start. The money and the facsimiles and the address. It was essential to have something to look forward to. He would do a good job. Marshall was right to trust him. The Turnbull sisters would get their money, Marshall would get his beastly stamps, and Jack and Sylvia would pay all the outstanding arrears, and survive. Agnes and Jeremy too. He loved all of them very much. One day, when they were out of debt, he would tell Sylvia, and arrange a treat for her, a trip to Mauritius perhaps. Was the local hotel in Port Louis still there?

17

The day after the visit of Sylvia and Jack, Marshall was too weak to see anyone. Dr Zilkha did several tests and said little about what he had learnt from them. As a director of the company which owned the clinic, it was useful to keep his patients alive as long as possible. The longer they lived, the longer they paid. Humanitarian and financial considerations were not, as they so often are, in opposition. Jane, who stayed loyally by Marshall's bed, inquired of the doctor what was the latest prognosis. The doctor said that he did not have one. Was Marshall weaker? Yes he was. Would the end come quickly? It might, especially if the condition were complicated by an infection. Were we talking in days, or weeks, or months? Not months.

But the following day, Marshall again seemed a little stronger. Jane asked for a basin and washed his thinning hair for him. She had been reading the Bible, but the more she read the more depressed she became. When she came to 2 Chronicles 21, she read of the squalid death of Jehoram, whose bowels fell out by reason of his sickness, and who died of sore diseases. 'And his people made no burning for him, like the burning of his fathers . . . and he reigned in Jerusalem eight years, and departed without being desired. Howbeit they buried him in the city of David, but not in the sepulchres of the kings.' She put away the Bible for a while after this, and so postponed reading about the wickedness of King Ahaziah and the revolt against Athaliah and the loving life of Jehoiada and the tragedy of Uzziah, who did such splendid work to glorify the Lord, but then trespassed by burning incense which was only permitted to be burnt by the sons of Aaron, and maybe as a result became suddenly leprous in his forehead and was thrust out.

Instead she read a paperback. It advanced the affecting story of a country magistrate and the daughter of his best friend, whom he brings up as his own daughter, after the best friend, a pilot in the RAF, is reported missing, believed killed. But, as Jane had expected, the dead pilot turns out not to be dead after all, and returns, much altered, and with amnesia, to Blighty, where, falling on hard times, he is rescued from the bottle by the good offices of the charitable young woman, whom he fails to recognise as his daughter. The romantic and provocative entanglements which the ingenious writer had invented for her protagonists were more to Jane's taste than Athaliah, Jehoiada and the rest, and succeeded in keeping her mind temporarily from Dr Zilkha's gloomy prognostications.

While Jane washed his hair, Amelia made the bed with the linen sheets which were one of the most desirable features of the clinic. All of these women who surround him, Jane thought, and minister to him, and not one of us would he settle down with. She had known something of his association with Jacqueline, and had guessed at more, but the extent of his desolation was beyond her comprehension. She had never expected that Marshall would settle down with an older woman, or such a beautiful one. If only he had been a Battle of Britain pilot with amnesia and a drinks problem, or even a country magistrate, someone would have come along. But he had leprosy in his forehead and was cast out . . .

Marshall asked Jane for Stacey Anne; also for his attaché case. When Jane arrived with both, Marshall took a bundle of notes out of the case and handed the money to Jane.

'Nothing in my will,' he whispered to her. 'Better have this now. Stop the buzzards getting their hands on it. Now go away and put it in a safe place before I change my mind.'

18

*M*et a gal in calico down in Santa Fe,
Used to be her Sunday beau 'till I rode away
Do I want her, do I want her love? Yes siree!
Will I win her, will I win her love? wait 'n' see!
Workin' with a Rodeo, go from town to town,
See most every kind of gal, every kind of gown,
But who made my heart sing? Yippee Yi Yippee Yo!
My little gal in calico.

The songs were a part of the ritual which Marshall devised
for the sorting of stamps. It was to become an essential
accompaniment. Marshall would arrive back at the apartment
and set out the packets and stock books on a large Pembroke
table with a dark green cloth. To one side of him the
ultraviolet lamps, the mounts, the tweezers, the magnifiers.
To the other the albums, in order as he was most likely to need
them, and reference books. The songs he had meticulously
copied on to long-play tapes, and as meticulously identified.
'A Gal in Calico', recorded by Carmen Cavallaro and his
orchestra with vocal refrain, was typical of the songs Marshall
liked best, maudlin, sentimental pieces with pretty tunes,
although he favoured them particularly when sung by female
singers, Deanna Durbin, Judy Garland, Rosemary Clooney.

On a separate table (in case of accidents) a bottle of wine and a glass. Unlike the music, the wine would be selected for its appropriateness to the stamps. An Australian Sauvignon would accompany the demanding business of examining the Australian 'Roo issues with their exacting shades and dyes and watermark varieties. A rough retsina would have to do when it came to sorting the Greek Hermes Heads, and rum for the Jamaicans.

Once he had started the music and opened the wine and set out the accessories he could start on the work itself.

The carton had contained possibly a hundred thousand stamps. None was dated after the mid-Twenties, and most were from the nineteenth century. Many of the more significant country collections contained first issues, either mint, or used, or occasionally both. These he carefully transferred into the appropriate stock book having tested them for authenticity and flaws. Almost all of the stamps proved to be genuine, although at the time Marshall did not recognise how unusual this was. Whoever had put this accumulation together must have had a keen eye, a wide knowledge and a fat purse.

The problem then arose as to how best to dispose of the highly desirable remaindered stamps. This was where Marcel had come in handy. He had taken what Marshall had no further use for and supplied in exchange the first issues of the countries Marshall lacked. Until the Portuguese event, very little money had changed hands. About their business arrangements Marcel had been enigmatically Gallic.

'We are friends, are we not, and friends trust one another, I think. We are not (what is the phrase I seek for?) pen-pushers.'

Such sentiments, expressed with many a wrinkled smile, a raised eyebrow and a wry shrug, were irresistible. Marshall suspected that Marcel had done marvellously well out of their association, but his knowledge of philatelic matters was so severely limited that he could never be sure. He did know that

Marcel had never palmed him off with rubbish. When Marshall had the collection valued, the expert commented on what beautiful examples he had acquired, and 'beauty' was a word that cropped up more and more when Marshall sorted his stamps. They *were* beautiful, perhaps because of their honesty. Latterly stamps were produced by greedy countries with the requirements of dealers in the forefront of their minds. The simple process of posting a letter was no longer paramount. Greed and self-consciousness had taken over from naïf artistry. Who really wanted to stick vulgar reproductions of Rubenesque nudes on their envelopes? Things became so decadent that some countries seemed to have no raison d'être other than to issue stamps. The Tongans issued weirdly shaped stamps like jigsaw pieces, or blatantly coloured ones like luggage labels, or circular ones like gold coins.

But in the first issues, patriotism, dignified symbolism, a flair for colour and a delight in the crafts of engraving and printing combined to produce, not just beauty, but rare beauty. Take the first issues from Nova Scotia as an example. Squared or diamond-shaped, they combined the young Queen, her crown, the heraldic flowers of the United Kingdom and the mayflower of Nova Scotia into such elaborate and beautiful tracery as to dazzle the imagination, while the colours of the first imperforate issue, red-brown, deep blue, bright blue, pale blue, yellow-green, deep green, cold violet, deep purple and purple, in the values from a penny to a shilling, were graduated with such subtlety as to make them worth every penny (and they amounted to several million pennies) which Marshall had had to pay for them.

So Marshall passed his unwanted stamps to Marcel and others, who, in the time-honoured tradition of stamp collectors, swapped them for the rare and wonderful stamps Marshall did want, and Marshall's collection became closer and closer to completion, and the singers sang on.

I took a trip on the train
and I thought about you
I passed a shadowy lane
and I thought about you.
Two or three cars parked under the stars,
A winding stream,
Moon shining down on the same little town,
And with each beam,
Same old dream.
At every stop that we made
Oh, I thought about you,
But when I pulled down the shade,
Then I really felt blue.
I peeked through the crack and looked at the track,
The one going back to you,
And what did I do?
I thought about you!

The plangent harmonies of the music always brought back the same face to Marshall's memory. The face and the voice and the perfume. The perfume and the body. He could not order a meal without thinking, What would Jacqueline have had? He could not see a film without wondering, Would she have approved? The cheap music sharpened the pain and the stamps eased it. He had found a way of coping.

19

Stacey Anne breezed into the room as though life was a perpetual holiday and every day was summer. She wore a sleeveless cotton frock printed with audaciously large lilies, and had an absurd piece of ribbon in her hair.

'A beautiful day,' she said, and twirled as though in a Scottish reel. 'I'm off to Carcassonne in a week, so whatever it was you wanted to see me about had better not have long-term implications.'

'I understand. Jane, would you mind leaving us?'

'I would mind very much,' said Jane, 'not that my feelings matter.' None the less she took as long as she could packing away her knitting into her tapestry bag. 'I'm about as much use as a clothes brush to a Zulu warrior.' She was becoming increasingly crotchety and increasingly fanciful. But she did what she was told, though for how much longer was questionable.

Then in a weak voice, and with several pauses for oxygen, Marshall told Stacey Anne about his brother-in-law, and the mission he was on in Wakefield.

'You already know how important the outcome of all this is to me. The trouble is, I just don't trust Jack. He's off tomorrow. I want you to follow him and report back.'

'Has he met me?'

'I don't think so.'

'And how will I know him?'

'I've booked him a room at the Griffin in Leeds. It's not a big place. If you stay there too . . . Well, the rest is up to you.'

'What are you most afraid of, Marshall?'

'That he'll run off with the money. Or the stamps.'

'Has he taken a lot of money?'

'Yes. Not everything I have but a large part of it. It should be enough to buy the stamps. Anything over he keeps.'

'And it's down to me, using my Celtic wiles, to stop him running off. Is that the sort of thing you had in mind?'

'The sort of thing.'

'And now I've something to tell you, Marshall. You know that French friend of yours, the one who has such a way with a girl?'

'Marcel.'

'Well, he's got me in the family way. So what do you think to that?'

Marshall knew exactly what he felt. It wasn't an emotion he had expected to feel again. He felt jealous.

20

Jack had taken most of Marshall's cash and had gone to Wakefield and Stacey Anne had gone after him. Marshall could do nothing but await the reports which the two had promised to file, Jack at eight each evening, Stacey Anne at nine. He was too tired to worry.

The chaplain came to see him. Jane barred his way.

'You'll get nowhere with him. You're wasting your time.'

The chaplain looked like an ageing footballer with massive shoulders, a crew cut and a face of salacious innocence.

'Scarcely wasting my time, I think. It's what I'm here for.'

'What? To keep dying men from their needful rest?'

The chaplain looked pained. 'That's a rather partial description of what I do. My job is to bring comfort to troubled souls.'

'How do you know they're troubled? And how do they know what comfort you've brought them when they reckon up your pay cheque?'

'May I at least speak to Mr Marshall, and find out from his own lips that he has no need of my services?'

'It's not my place to stop you, merely to warn you that you won't be welcome. However if you were female and twenty years younger . . .'

Marshall's eyes were closed, but his eyelids flickered when he heard the dulcet tones of the bullet-headed divine.

'I am a man of God, and I am employed by the clinic to minister to souls in torment.'

Jane snorted derisively, and Marshall gave a grunt, which might have been interpreted as disapproval.

'Told you,' said Jane.

'I am here to give you the balm of Gilead.'

Marshall's eyes, sunk deeper in his face since he had entered the clinic, flickered open.

'Do you collect stamps?'

The chaplain chuckled. 'That is not a question I get asked very often, but as it happens I have for several years now subscribed to the Post Office's first day cover service. A very engaging pastime.'

'Marshall hates modern stamps,' said Jane.

'In that case perhaps he would like to talk about matters spiritual.'

'I doubt it,' said Jane.

'Come closer and sit down,' Marshall grunted.

The chaplain, who had been hovering by the bed, did as he was told and breathed peppermint-flavoured mouthwash into the face of the man he was employed to save from the terrors of eternal damnation.

Marshall gestured to Jane to leave them. 'Bloody corridors again,' she grunted as she left.

'What's the worst thing you've ever done?' Marshall asked the chaplain.

'That's not such a straightforward question as your previous one. And much depends on what you mean by worst.'

'It's what you mean by worst,' said Marshall.

'Well, in that case I suppose it would have to be a sin of commission, rather than omission, and not so much the withholding of love as the active participation in hate. I was a bully in my Army days. We drove a young recruit to despair.'

'And?'

'He left the Army, and I found Christ.'

'He had the best of the bargain.'

'I think not.'

'It sounds to me as though you saved him, and lost yourself. Myself, I have withheld love, and participated in hate, and even murder.'

The chaplain was taken aback. At the same time he was well aware that saving the soul of a murderer would look excellent on his curriculum vitae. A serious business therefore, but one hell of a challenge.

'When was this murder?'

'Tomorrow perhaps, or the next day. And maybe not at all.'

Here was a puzzle worthy of the Delphic Oracle. How could a dying man confined within a clinic be about to commit a murder? Clearly it was intended as a metaphor. Or, most probably, he was referring to himself. This unfortunate fellow was contemplating suicide. What a challenge!

'Not at all, I beg of you. You must not succumb. God in his infinite mercy measures all things, including the length of our days.'

As the chaplain droned on, speaking inspiringly of the love of God, and His miraculous interventions in human affairs, which included of course, the sending down of Jesus Christ, His only begotten Son, to take upon himself the sins of man, Marshall's breathing became regular and his eyes closed. The chaplain had not brought him the comfort of divine mercy, but the more immediately accessible and enjoyable comfort of sleep, untroubled by dreams.

21

The Turnbull sisters were not unused to being approached by ambitious philatelists waving cheque books. After a story in *Philatelist Monthly* about their astonishing collection, there had been regular inquiries. Those who wrote and asked to see the stamps received their letters back hand-stamped: NOT KNOWN AT THIS ADDRESS. In years to come, these very envelopes were destined to become collector's items in their own right. Those who telephoned were politely told by one or other of the sisters that both had gone abroad and would not return from their round-the-world cruise for many months. Only Marshall's inquiry had received their sympathetic attention, because of his celebrated father.

'I admired that man,' said Susan, the elder sister.

'So did I, dear,' said Martha. 'He saved us from Rommel.'

'I liked him on the radio. He always talked such good sense.'

'And he always knew the answers. And this is his son?'

'He claims to be, dear. And why should he make a false claim which must become palpably transparent were we to meet him?'

'Nothing can be palpably transparent.'

'Why yes, dear, it can. Window glass can, and perspex, and untruths, very nearly.'

When Marshall failed to show himself, the sisters were

bemused and disappointed.

'I do hope so much that he has not suffered an accident on the way,' said Susan.

'Indeed, dear, I hope so too, especially since he had warned us that he is not in the best of health.'

The following day, Jane, acting on her own initiative, had telephoned the sisters to apologise for Marshall's non-appearance, and to blame the pile-up on the M1. The sisters had heard about it on the radio. Marshall would very much like to reschedule the visit, Jane averred, as soon as his health permitted him to make a second attempt.

'But –' she continued severely, 'that could be some considerable time away.'

Mollified, the sisters had put the bottle of tonic back on the shelf, and eaten the home-made scones.

Jack rang at eight. The telephone was on a trolley at Marshall's bedside. Marshall had been dreaming of a lunar landscape with volcanoes, out of whose declivities a series of heads came popping with unseemly regularity. The faces on the heads were the faces of women he had known, and they stretched their necks upwards until they dominated the landscape, then turned their heads spasmodically like chickens. There was Jane and Stacey Anne, Jacqueline, and the one who thought he was in advertising, and Corinne, only something was wrong with her (it could have been the moustache). What was Marshall's role? Was he an independent observer, or the moon itself? Like a pomander stuck with cloves.

'Marshall? I've checked in. And I've hired a car, just a Metro, nothing fancy, because I know you're concerned about the cash. And I'm keeping a record of everything, so there needn't be any unpleasantness about it when I get back. I had a haircut too, at a place across the way, because I thought if it came to it, you know, I wanted to make a good impression. Italian boys, Carlo and Mario, very friendly. And I've checked the Turnbull residence. Lights were on, but I'm waiting till the morning before I make contact. That seems characteristic of furniture restorers. Should I mention your name to them, Marshall?'

'No.'

'Right. Right. No problem there. Anything else you need to know?'

'Nothing.'

'Same time tomorrow.'

'Yes.'

Stacey Anne rang at nine.

'How long has he got, Dr Zilkha?'

'That is the question we never answer. We can give a best-and worst-case analysis, but it's of little value, now we are near the end. There is jaundice and weight loss. Have you noticed any mental deterioration?'

'He says less and less. I think he is frightened. I nursed his father too. But he died of a heart attack.'

'We all do in a way.'

Dr Zilkha realised he had no idea of the woman's name, nor of her status, which was obviously low.

'I think, dear lady,' he said, 'that we are no longer talking of months, and possibly not even of weeks. The patient had been stable for some time. There has recently been evidence of accelerating damage to the vital organs. But the most important variable is the will of the patient. Temporary remission is not uncommon but people die when they choose to die, when it becomes preferable to hanging on. In my experience, it is usually a pleasurable option. Like: shall I have another of these excellent sandwiches? No, on the whole I have enjoyed a sufficiency. The question you must ask is: how much does he have to live for? The answer to that question is the answer to your question. Have you considered what you will do after the time has come for him?'

Jane smiled, and sipped her China tea. She had acquired a taste for it since she had been attending the clinic.

'Yes,' she said. 'There is nothing for me to do.'

Marshall, who had been dozing for most of the day, became sharply conscious at the hour of Jack's anticipated call. When no call came, he grew fractious. There was no call either, an hour later, when Stacey Anne was expected to ring. He pestered Jane to contact the hotel they were staying in. She asked him for the name. He could not remember it. He called her an incompetent idiot. The Scandinavian woman had to force him to take his sleeping pills, and, even after he had swallowed them, he lay rigid in his bed, his yellowing eyes staring fiercely out at a treacherous world.

22

'You must know something,' said Sylvia. 'It's easy enough for you lying in that big bed, waited on hand and foot, and pretending to be asleep.'

'I think he *is* asleep, Sylvia dear,' said Jane.

Sylvia was not to be placated. Her anger was entirely without artifice, just as her love was. In that respect, Jack had been fortunate in his choice.

Marshall sighed and opened his eyes.

'I'm not asleep. I wish I was.'

'So where is he then? He comes home, packs a bag, leaves me the housekeeping in fifty-pound notes so that I *know* something is up, says he's going to be away for a few days, that he's on a commission from you, and that he'll be in touch. That was last Wednesday, Marshall, and since then nothing. I've got his bloody business manager (which in my opinion is a contradiction in terms) hassling me, I've got the bank hassling me, I've got the kids asking impossible questions, and here's you living the life of Riley and saying you wish you were asleep. Frankly, Marshall, it's not good enough!'

'It's stamps,' said Jane. 'He sent Jack off to buy stamps for him, although to my way of thinking he's got more than enough of the things already.'

'Buying stamps? How long does it take to buy stamps? And

what's Jack living on all this time? I'm sure I don't know what *I* am.'

'The trouble with women,' Marshall announced, and from either side of the bed Jane and Sylvia looked at each other in surprise. 'The trouble with women is that they're always in the right. You know bloody everything, don't you? Florence Nightingale was in the right. Bloody Marie Stopes was in the right. It may turn out that Margaret Thatcher was right too all along. Well Sylvia, if you're so clever, you go and find Jack yourself. He's staying in a hotel in Leeds, or was, and no, I can't remember the name of it, because I'm a man and because I'm dying, which are two excellent excuses for my incompetence, right?'

Although Marshall was exhausted by this speech, and had to clamp his jaw to endure the stab of pain in his chest and upper back – the pain that was always there, sitting inside him like a cat, ready at any moment to open its claws and scratch – he was proud of it too. He had only been trying to help Jack, and Sylvia, just as she had asked him to. Who did she think she was?

'I will check the hotels in Leeds,' said Sylvia. 'And cross my fingers that there's a straightforward explanation. If not –' she paused and gave Marshall one of her winsome smiles – 'don't expect to see me at your funeral!'

Two days after Sylvia's visit, Harry Nissen called. His characteristic geniality was missing, and he wasted no time on preliminary niceties. Jane, who had become a fixture, knitting shapeless and nameless articles beside Marshall's bed, stood up to block his passage, but Harry sidestepped her with some agility. He was waving at Marshall a page torn from a newspaper.

'Look at this? Will ye bloody look at this, man?'

'Can't you see the poor lamb is dying?' Jane muttered, wishing she had a stronger argument to put to this rude Scotsman.

'Aye, and aren't we all? And some of us –' he waved the paper in the old woman's face '– violently.'

'You're a rude man,' said Jane, and, since there seemed little she could do to influence events, she resumed her knitting.

Marshall's eyes were open. 'Oh, it's you, Harry,' he said. 'Will you have a grape?'

'Those poor women! Have ye not heard?'

Since Marshall clearly had not, Harry read the cutting to him. It concerned the Turnbull sisters of Wakefield who had been, as the reporter put it, disturbed by an intruder, and battered to death, possibly with a poker, although no murder weapon was found on the scene. The sisters, aged seventy-seven and seventy-nine, had lived on their own in a large house, which had belonged to their father, a prominent mill owner. The motive for the murder was a mystery. The sisters had not been sexually molested, and there was no evidence of robbery. The local police, who had set up a helpline, which members of the public should call if they had seen anything suspicious, confessed themselves baffled. Harry grabbed hold of Marshall's pyjamas, and pulled him upright until the two were face to face.

'Did you have a hand in this, eh? Because if you did . . .'

'Careful of the drip,' Jane warned, for the stand was rattling ominously.

'What harm did they ever do to you?'

Marshall smiled slightly. 'Not me . . .' he croaked.

'Well I shall go and talk to the police, and I shall ask them to look see if there aren't some albums of stamps about the place; and if there are I shall ask them to turn to Mauritius, in case mebbe there are some gaps on the page – you know to what I am referring, eh? Dying, indeed! Ye'll not die until we've sorted this little matter out, I think.' Harry slumped down on the bed. 'It's a sad day. Why did ye no let me get the stamps for you? I would have done it without all this sad palaver.' He paused, and absent-mindedly took a grape. 'If the stamps are all there, they'll be coming on to the market, I suppose. That's a thought, eh? Will you make it worth my while not to bid against you, Marshall?'

'What a terrible man,' said Jane, 'making all those rude insinuations. I shall instruct them downstairs that on no account are they to let him in again.'

'Thank you, Jane.'

'And one other thing. You're supposed to go to the Palace next month for this investiture thing. I rang them – me! – and explained to them that you were a bit poorly just now, and they said not to worry, and they'll have one of those chair things waiting, if you're up to it, so I'll get your morning suit out of mothballs, shall I, and have a go with the Dabitoff.'

23

Marshall drifted between reality and dream. On his computer display there had been a furry ball which had bounced endlessly between the angles of the screen, never losing pace or energy, but never achieving anything, a precise analogue, Marshall had thought, for his work at the Treasury. Now he had become that ball, buffeted between the real world, which daily seemed less real, and his fantasies, which were increasingly seductive.

But there were landmarks in this ceaseless voyage: there was day and night, and Marshall became obsessed with the need to know the time whenever he returned to consciousness. He could raise his wrist slightly from the sheets and turn his head towards it; but sometimes the effort of focusing his eyes was too great for him. He became especially concerned to know how long there was to go before eight, then before nine at night. The other landmark was his stamp albums. Jane had placed them on a table within his line of vision. At his request she would open one and flip through the pages until one country caught his eye, the Romantic Swiss Cantonals, the delightful Ball Bay Pictorials of Norfolk Island, the weirdly named Portuguese Colonial overprints of Inhambane, Tete and Quelimane. Once, by mistake, Jane opened the page at Mauritius. Marshall howled at her.

The pain was less now, or his resistance to it greater. Were they drugging him? No one answered when he asked. But if they were not, surely they would tell him that they were not, instead of this infuriating prevarication.

One day the police came to see him; a detective chief inspector and a sergeant. It was one of Marshall's brighter days, but the policemen seemed inhibited. They had authority over everyone with whom they had to deal. Top City businessmen, cabinet ministers, clergymen; they could drag them out of bed and put them through the old one-two. But in the presence of mortality they became subdued, and spoke softly, even respectfully. It was the chase that excited them, not the kill. The agent who killed Dillinger killed himself years later with the same gun.

They said that they were investigating the murder of the Turnbull sisters. Marshall nodded his head. They said that they were following up every lead, but to be candid, they had very little to go on. They said that the sisters had written Marshall's name in an appointments book by the telephone; had he been to visit them about a week before their tragic demise? Jane intervened to say that he had intended to, he had even tried to, but traffic on the motorway . . .

The policemen sympathised; the traffic was terrible these days. They told an amusing anecdote about a recent car chase in which both the criminals and the pursuing guardians of the law had become enmeshed in the same hold-up.

What had been the purpose of Marshall's intended visit to Wakefield? Marshall managed to answer the question. He had been in touch with the sisters about some stamps he was interested in acquiring.

Stamps. Fascinating. They had found a large collection in the sisters' house, and since it was clearly of some value, they had scratched their heads over why it had not been taken by the murderers. Bludgeoning those old ladies to death, and no motive for doing so; it was a real conundrum.

Was the collection intact, Marshall wondered. Intact? What did that mean? A jigsaw puzzle with a piece missing, one could identify at a glance that all was not as it should be. But a stamp collection . . .?

Maybe, if they showed it to him, Marshall suggested . . . But out of Marshall's sightlines Jane was shaking her head at the policemen. Not a good idea. As things stood at present not at all a good idea.

Anyway, said the senior policeman, they had ruled burglary out as a motive for the crime. They were not interested in the stamps. The sisters had died intestate. The police thought there might be some relative of the sisters who stood to gain from their death, although they had not been able to trace any. If there was such a relative, he or she had better think twice before coming to claim his or her inheritance. They would be waiting for him or her. Crank calls, said the sergeant, as they prepared to leave, that was one of the crosses the police had to bear in a case such as this, crank calls. They were thinking of employing a PR firm to weed out the nutters. Or pass them straight to the Samaritans, chuckled the chief inspector. Both policemen found this suggestion amusing.

The visit of the police in connection with the Wakefield murders had a distressing consequence. Dr Zilkha told Marshall that they were no longer willing to accommodate him at the clinic.

Jane became apoplectic. Why on earth not? There was no suggestion that Marshall was in any way implicated in the murders. How could he be, a dying man? Of course Dr Zilkha realised that, but he was simply not prepared to have the police, uniformed or plain-clothes, walking around the clinic. It lowered morale amongst the staff, and could have disastrous implications for the profitable running of the place.

'We'll loan him the use of an ambulance to take him wherever he wants to go. No charge.'

'Washing your hands of him?'

Dr Zilkha said: 'One of the mysteries of Christianity is how you came to make a villain out of Pilate. He always seemed to me to behave with impeccable correctness.'

'Why not just kill him off and have done with it?' Jane asked, regretting the remark as soon as she had uttered it. She regretted it because it would do nothing to heal the breach, and also because if she refused to allow Marshall to be moved, there was no way she could ensure that they did not do exactly as she had suggested. But where was he to go?

Sylvia suggested that he should move in with her. Since Jack had gone – well, wherever he *had* gone – and with the children at school and college, she was alone in the house. If Marshall paid her what he had been paying the clinic, the disastrous financial situation Jack had left behind him would at least be temporarily eased.

'I'm not sure about that, Sylvia dear,' said Jane. 'I think his Private Patients Plan has been paying for all this. He had a special sort of one, you see. I don't think he was paying anyway. On the other hand I think that maybe the policy has expired.'

The women looked at each other across Marshall's recumbent figure.

'Well, he'll have to pay something,' said Sylvia. 'I'm not a charity. So either he moves into his apartment, which he couldn't manage anyway, no matter how good you are with him, or my place, or the street.'

'The two apartments were on a lease,' said Jane. 'It's up this year.'

'If all else fails,' said Sylvia with a touch of malice, 'we can always sell his stamps.'

Jane did not accompany Marshall and Sylvia in the ambulance. She had returned to Marshall's apartments to discuss arrangements with the landlords. It was clear that Marshall would never be returning to his home.

'When he dies, we have no further problems,' said the

landlord's representative. 'But until then there is the tiresome matter of the outstanding rent . . .'

'And if it isn't paid?'

'Goods to the value of. We'll take possession of the two apartments, and set the contents against the debt.'

'But those things are worth a fortune. His treasures. Lovely things.'

'Sentimental value. The eyes of love are blind. It's a case of what the market can stand. Our bailiffs are experienced fellows.'

'Perhaps I should sell them on his behalf. Except that they are not mine to sell.'

'You will have to move fast, madam. I've called in the bailiffs for Wednesday week.'

'That's the day he's going to the Palace for his investiture.'

'He will be ennobled and impoverished all at once then,' chuckled the loathsome landlord's agent. 'All part of life's rich tapestry.'

24

At Sylvia's house Agnes and Jeremy had prepared the spare room against Marshall's arrival at the weekend. Although it was still referred to as the spare room, it had been Jack's room for some years. Increasingly often, Jack, guilty of various misdemeanours, some venal, some heinous, had been banished to it, until it became exceptional for him to share the marriage bed. However, decorum required that the room still be referred to as the 'spare room'; and so it was.

Jeremy had bought a bunch of daffodils and placed them in a milk bottle beside the bed. He and Agnes had been told by their mother that Jack was away on a business trip. Ten days had passed. Agnes suspected that her father had been arrested. Several times in recent months men in tight suits with short hair and large shoes had visited the house and been closeted with Jack. These 'business associates' left without the polite formalities, and grim-faced. There was much not spoken of in the Bexleyheath household to which the ambulance brought Marshall. Would Jack be returning? If so, when? Was Marshall dying? If so, when? Did Sylvia have expectations? If so, what? Why had Marshall left the clinic? If Jack returned before Marshall died, who would sleep where?

Agnes, who had just started a psychology course at Aston University as a possible alternative to giving herself to Christ, was intrigued. Were all households like this? If so, why were the television soap operas so dull and uneventful? She discussed the household and its tensions with her youthful tutor, pretending that it was happening to 'a friend'. The tutor asked her to write an essay in which she predicted how a) the uncle's death, and b) the father's return, would affect the status quo.

Jeremy asked his mother whether there was anything he could do to help. At the third time of asking she told him with a touch of asperity to do his homework.

'You never visited us here, Marshall,' Sylvia said, as the ambulance drew up in the anonymous street. 'Five years we've lived here, and you never once came. Don't blame you. But it would have helped to prepare you for the shock. Among other things.'

As the ambulance driver and Jeremy helped him through the door, Agnes emerged in a tennis dress, swinging a racket. That was a greater shock, and one for which Marshall was entirely unprepared.

25

The packet from Stacey Anne arrived three days later, just as Sylvia was leaving for the adult education class she tutored. It carried a Denver, Colorado postmark.

'There's a letter for you, Marshall,' Sylvia said. 'I'll bring it up to you when I get back.'

From the bed Marshall had a view across a cluster of fields to a conference centre. It had the appearance of Jonah's gourd which grew up in a night to perish in a night. Within it executives were trained in mysteriously invented simulations on such arcane topics as iconography and consumer ethics. Outside real consumers trudged across those same fields from council flat to allotment. Jeremy said he had done a school project on the town, and beneath the allotments was a plague pit. One evening Marshall saw two schoolchildren making love there under a leering moon.

'I wonder if it's possible,' Jeremy mused, 'that the great plagues were an early form of AIDS. Do you know we get AIDS instruction before we get sex education? But we get drugs and smoking and road safety before AIDS instruction. They terrify us out of innocence.'

Jeremy enjoyed chatting to Marshall, whose silence was refreshingly non-judgemental in a world in which, as he put it, 'Everyone Knows Best'. He had also interested himself in

Marshall's stamp collection, which Jane had brought in a taxi. But the bonsai tree had been abandoned in the clinic.

'It's not just the designs and the colours of the old sets,' he said, 'but what you told me about how they kept the same stamps in use for a decade or more. Why does everything have to move so fast these days? Some football clubs have half a dozen strips a year.'

For Marshall, things moved slowly. At his most clear-headed he was determined to cling on to the sensations of each moment. The taste of fruits and salads, the circulation of air when his window was thrust open in the mornings, the scent of flowers. But such pleasures were increasingly sporadic, and he was pulled away from them into semi-coma, like a passenger in a boat that was being towed away from a familiar shoreline.

'I'd better read you the letter,' said Sylvia, whose helpfulness was spiced with curiosity. Marshall had read one addressed to her nearly forty years before, although she had never known about it.

'Shall I?'

Marshall nodded.

Sylvia removed it from its flimsy paper. 'It isn't a letter at all. It's a tape. There's a note wrapped around it. It says: "Having a great time. Wish you were here. Love Stacey Anne."'

'Play it.'

26

Marshall – hey, it's grand to speak to you again after so long. I've missed you. Does that surprise you as much as it surprises me? Hope you're still alive by the way. You probably are. Dr Z is really good at keeping patients alive. It's as if his life depended on it.

I think I owe you a tape, and probably an apology as well, because I promised to telephone you regularly. I was going to, but Jack said that in the circumstances –

Sylvia, who was ironing shirts by the bed, pressed the pause button on the machine.

From the distant allotments a dog barked. It had unearthed a bone of impressive dimensions, large enough to be human.

'What's this about Jack? Is it my Jack? And what's she to do with Jack?'

'Be quiet,' whispered Marshall. 'I need to hear this.'

– So anyway, there we were in Leeds, and I did get to know Jack as you'd suggested I should. He was rather sweet to me that first night and we had a high old time. He had all these fifty-pound notes, d'you see, and they were burning a hole in his pocket, I fancy. So we went and had a steak, which was terrific, really raw and tender with all the trimmings, and then Jack took me to this night club where there were these shameless hussies showing everything God gave them to anyone who cared to look, and would you believe it, one of them was Fidelina Mulkere who won the Darlin' Girls from Clare competition.

Remember? I asked her how she was getting on, and she said not so bad really, and would I like to work in the club 'cos the money was great, and I told her that if I wanted to show off my fanny, I would be a bit careful about who I showed it to, and that made Jack laugh, and he said something about being good at keeping his eyes open and his mouth shut, and I said what about his wallet, and then he bought us all pina coladas, which are a kind of Spanish cocktail served with an umbrella on top to keep out the rainwater, I suppose, and then we tried our luck in the casino.

Again Sylvia pressed the pause button. Marshall muttered crossly. The sunlight lay across the quilted bed and particles of dust, scarcely heavier than air, floated through it.

'Jane rang me,' she said. 'You were asleep and we thought it better not to wake you. They are going to take possession of your flat – both flats in fact – and the contents. Jane said she couldn't cope and she's moved to a niece in Hebden Bridge. Did you know she had one? I didn't. She says if you need her, she'll pop down at once. I got the impression that she wasn't too fit. It's her ninety-second birthday today, she said. I sent her some soap and stuff and a card from us both. I didn't even know which day her birthday was, did you? leave alone her age. She said she'd quite like to take you to the investiture if you're up to it. And if she is. But I don't think she will be. I'm not at all sure I want to hear the rest of this tape, do you, Marshall?'

But she stayed, and they did.

Well Jack turned out to be a really nice guy, but when I asked him what he was doing in Leeds on a wet Tuesday, he said that was a secret, but he had come up north to clinch a deal, and I asked him what sort of a deal, but of course what Jack didn't know was that I already knew what sort of a deal, but I wasn't going to let on that I knew. Didn't I do well, Marshall? But hey, that was just the beginning!

So what happened then was that we had some more pina coladas until they asked us to leave, because of police regulations, and Jack asked Fidelina (who he called Fiddly because he said he would like to fiddle with her, so she said she would call him Jerk not Jack and then he could jerk off to his heart's content) if she'd like to come back to the Griffin with us for a snifter, but I shook my head at her, and she said that it was very decent of Jack to ask her but that she had to get her beauty sleep if it was all the same to him, so. When Fidelina's had a few she sounds like she's never left Clare at all, and I wouldn't be surprised if she doesn't come to wish she never had, the way she's carrying on. But then again, I suppose I can't really talk, can I?

'When we were children,' said Sylvia, 'I thought you were God. I'd have done anything you asked me to, Marshall. I used to have fantasies that you would ask me to do impossible things, like jump out of a tall tower, or swim the Channel, and I would do them without a murmur. I couldn't bear it when people bad-mouthed you. When you went off to boarding-school I would sleep in your bed sometimes. Did you know? I would move things around, just a tadge, to see if you noticed. Did you? You never mentioned it. What happened to change it all? You froze me out, Marshall. You never answered my prayers. You never set me impossible tasks. I know how Jane must feel. I had to marry Jack, you see, to break the fetters. Each time you said how strongly you disapproved I could hear the chains snapping. I was so happy.'

Now I expect you're wondering, if you're still listening – and I hope you are because the most interesting bits are still to come – what about Marcel, and what I expect you'd call my 'interesting condition'. Well, Marshall dear, I'm afraid that was a bit of a porkie. As you know we did have our night of passion in the Carcassonne, but though the nuns may have been remiss in some ways, they were real demons on the subject of birth control. One thing which I didn't pick up from the nuns, is that it's a great crack to tell fellas that you're up the spout, because it tends to turn them from ravening beasts into hunted animals, in my experience. Not you, Marshall, of course.

So there we are in Jack's hotel room in the Griffin, and he asks me what I'm doing in Leeds, and I say to mind his own business, and I bet I could guess what sort of a deal he was hoping to clinch. And he put money on the table next to the booze from the mini-bar, and I said I guessed it was something to do with the Post Office and it was, wasn't it? – sorry Marshall, but it all comes right in the end! – and he went a bit white, and admitted that in a way, it was. And I went on from there, 'guessing' right all the time, and he said that I should be a student of psychology, and I said, 'Clever of you, because that's just what I am, and that's what I'm doing in Leeds.'

So after that, he had little choice, but to tell Auntie Stacey Anne everything, and I rewarded him in the way I thought he would appreciate most, and also because he'd spent such a lot of your money on Fidelina and me, and not got a lot from it, except the worry that he'd been a bit indiscreet. Only I knew that whether he had been indiscreet or not didn't make a blind bit of difference when you get right down to it.

'Everything collapses in the end, doesn't it, Marshall? You, me, Jack, Jane, we will our own destruction. But what choices do we have? We can't stay in bed all our lives. We have to make decisions, move on, impinge on others. I wonder what Jane's niece in Hebden Bridge thinks about Jane moving in with her like that. We need to move on, but we shouldn't move on until we have finished our business, closed each chapter. Think of Daddy and those cartons. Guilty secrets. I suspected where they came from, by the way, but I was never entirely sure. I was justified in my suspicions. You took them over; the unfinished business. Did you have your suspicions? You must have, surely, yet you never let on. You thought you were cheating me, but God knows, the one who was being cheated was a civilisation away. You and your cartons and your stamps! Whatever happened to your divinity, Marshall?'

What was Jack like in the sack? Not a patch on Marcel, if you want the truth. You long for the gory details? Well, I'll give them to you, Marshall, if ever we meet again in this world or the next, but I am too shy to put biology on to this tape, and that's the truth of it. I mean anyone could get hold of this letter, even Sylvia dear. If you're listening, Sylvia dear, why does Jack smell of boot polish and did you *know he likes to have his balls sucked?*

Jack is better in a car than he is in bed. I think most men are. He handled that Metro like he was Ayrton Senna and the morning after the night before we bombed off to Wakefield and that tumbledown coffin of a place the Misses Turnbull called home. We've talked about it since, Jack and I, and we didn't have to bother with those two braying nanny-goats at all. We could have just skipped away with your money, but Jack does have a conscience and he said that he knew what those stamps meant to you, and he had given his word, and lots of stuff like that. I think we really meant to buy you the stamps, but one thing led to another, Marshall, and it's my experience of life that it usually does.

Did you know that the Turnbull sisters were Irish gels, eh? They come from Donegal. Did you know about Donegal? It's the northernmost part of Ireland so it's in the South. Magic. When I heard that lilt in their voices I could have hugged them both. But they weren't Catholics, that's for sure.

Jack had worked out some sort of story to tell them on the doorstep. He said should he be a brush salesman or a Mormon, but I said: 'Maybe they'll be happy to let you have the stamps, maybe they'll need the money, it looks like they could spend a bit on this place for starters.' I said: 'Be yourself, Jack.' I wish I hadn't said that, really because it was like a red rag to a bull. There was a long chain on the porch – a sort of up-market lavatory chain with a bell attached to it on the other side of the door. The sisters didn't have a butler or a maid or anything, and only a little yappy sort of dog which wouldn't have been any good in an emergency. What am I saying? It wasn't! So there we were standing on the porch and Jack talking about buying stamps from them, and representing you, Marshall, because you weren't well enough to travel, and the one who looked like a horse turning to the one who looked like a cow and saying: 'It's another of those beastly pests, dear.' And the one who looked like a cow said: 'Leave the chain on, dear!'

'Oh, come on ladies, give me a chance,' said Jack. 'I only want a couple of stamps, four at the most, and I'm absolutely loaded with

cash.'

And the horse-lady said that if Jack came from you, Marshall, he should have a letter to prove it, but that, even if he did have, they weren't going to let him in.

'How do we know,' said the cow-lady, 'that you haven't come here to beat our brains out, young man, and take whatever you like?'

I think it was hearing her say it, out loud like that, that gave Jack the idea. I know I felt a little thrill of excitement at just that moment, and I remembered Jack on top of me in bed, and that little ramrod of his.

'You don't,' said Jack, with a glance at me, and I could tell that he was thinking much the same as I was thinking. And he pushed hard against the door, and that chain, well, it was about as much use as an umbrella in a force-ten gale.

'Well, we've got a way of dealing with pests like you,' said the horse-woman, and reached into her big leather handbag. Did she have a gun or spray of some kind? What it was, apparently, was a special device that they'd given her down at the police station, a sort of alarm thing. All you did was press the button and lights started flashing at the cop-shop. But that sort of woman, well they don't know the simplest things, do they, because although she pressed the button, when I grabbed for it she dropped the device on the floor and it came open, and there weren't any batteries in it at all, at all. (You always liked me being a Darlin' Girl from Clare, didn't you, Marshall, with a bit of the old blarney, begorrah and bedad. Well, my begrandad was beaten to death by your Black and Tans, so make what you like outa that, me aul' feller. Plus I heard your dad say on the radio that the Irish were scum, that's the word he used, scum, and some people even applauded. Never forgot that, Marshall, never, not ever, though I was only a slip of a thing at the time.)

'I'll give you one last chance,' Jack said, which I thought was a bit cheeky of him, because it wasn't really for him to be giving them chances, being that they were minding their own business at home, and Jack was minding your business in Wakefield. 'You could at least negotiate. I'll offer you half a million for your Mauritius stamps, take

it or leave it.'

Half a million, I thought, he's finally flipped. They would take half that.

Then he spotted the cow-woman making a dash for the telephone, and he gave me the nod and I pulled it out of the wall, and the cow-woman gave a great moo, and sat down on the sofa with her plump legs sticking straight out in front of her, and the pooch, which had been very quiet up until then, started to yap, so Jack gave it a kick, and it flew through the air and ended up in the fire-grate . . .

Was Marshall still awake? He lay staring at the ceiling, his eyes unblinking, like a stone bishop in a cathedral. There should be rails around him; and of course, despite everything, there were. The hair had become quite fluffy around his great head, and quite white since he had entered the clinic; it framed his face like a mediaeval halo.

Ironic, Sylvia thought. I used to think he was God, and now he looks like Him.

The squalor of the taped narrative, and Stacey Anne's relish as she wittered on, scarcely affected Sylvia. Jack was lost to her. He had served his turn. Although Sylvia had stayed put, it was she who had moved on. Did she believe what she was hearing? Not entirely. Jack was capable of it; she imagined most men were capable of such excesses, but it was nothing to her. There would be plenty of time to concern herself with the consequences. The top priority was the protection of Agnes and Jeremy, as it always had been, but they were more of an age now to understand most things, even if they would find it hard to forgive. They already knew that Jack was a crook. They had been brought up in the knowledge that he had his own mysterious morality, which was little to do with what was current in Bexleyheath. If and when the details came out they would of course be shocked, but Agnes would try to analyse them, and the squirrel Jeremy would pack them away like nuts to be sorted out at a later stage.

After that it was mayhem, with the sisters keening, and Jack waving a poker about, warning them that if they didn't shut up and all that sort of thing, and then he hit one of them crack on the side of her head, and she put her hand up and said: 'Oh my Lord!' when she saw the blood, and the other one went for me with her nails, but I told her that it was nothing to do with me, and I had just come along for the ride, so to speak. Jack had really lost it by now, and was belaying about him in all directions, hitting anything that moved, and yelling out like he was in a Terminator film or something, even though Jack is no Arnie, is he, more's the pity.

I taped what happened then because I thought you'd be interested, Marshall, what with your generous investment and everything, but I'm afraid it didn't record properly because one of the Turnbull bitches gave it a great kick and must have damaged the mechanism in some way. Which is why I've recorded this on a rather superior American machine, as I think you'll agree when you hear my dulcet Irish burr. Plus, Marshall, I shan't charge you a penny extra because the way I reckon it is if it hadn't been for you I shouldn't be where I am today, which is Sitting Pretty Land.

So anyway there were the two old sisters, one of them gone quite grey, and the other one moaning and gurgling and spluttering and spewing up blood all over the Persian carpet, and I said to Jack: 'While we're here . . .' and Jack told me to see if I couldn't find the doo-dahs, and surprisingly I did. I mean if they were worth as much as you, Marshall, seem to think, why didn't they keep them in the bank, or at least locked in a safe (except that you don't either, do you?), but there they all were in a specially designed bookshelf. And I found Mauritius immediately after Malta. Meanwhile Jack was tidying things up a bit. There was a dustcover over the grand piano, and he put it over the sisters and their dog, like a shroud, and then I said: 'Give us a tune!' And he played 'Don't Cry for me Argentina', and he said it was in five flats, and I said, 'Wow!' and we both sang, except that that was the only line we could remember.

And then one of the sisters began caterwauling and grunting and groaning and calling us some really bad names which she ought not to have done in a situation like that and Jack asked should he, and I said

217

it was up to him, so then he fucked the one who was making all the racket and smacked her again with the poker, and that was her done for, but just in case he began cutting her up with a knife he found in the kitchen and he cut up the other one too, also the dog, and if you want to know what I was doing when all this was going on I had my feet up on the settee and I was nibbling at a bunch of grapes. True. Like Cleopatra or someone.

After that Jack had a really great idea, which was to take out the Mauritius Post Office stamps and put the facsimiles you'd given him in their place. They are beautiful, aren't they, all those stamps? I didn't have any idea until I saw them all together like that. So we'd got the stamps and the money, and the Misses Turnbull from Donegal had got their come-uppance, and so had the Black and Tans if you get what I'm driving at, and there's not really a lot more to tell. Bejasus.

We left the same day. Jack was nervous about clues, like fingerprints and such at the scene of the crime. It made me wonder whether his are on record somewhere. I told him not to be a big girl's blouse, and that if he had his passport with him we should get the hell out of the country. Which he did. Which we did. Looking back on it now, I wonder whether he'd expected that he'd need his passport or whether he'd just had it with him as a matter of course. Ask Sylvia about that if you're interested. She'll probably know, being the wife. Good old Sylvia. So we went to Manchester Airport and got on the first plane to leave for somewhere interesting, which turned out to be Madrid. And then we came here to America, which is quite a country, I can tell you, especially when you've got money.

I'm going to post this now. Jack has been drinking a bit, I'm afraid, and he's feeling the worse for wear, so I've left him asleep in the Best Western Hotel in Denver, the Mile High City.

Maybe Jack's got an altitude problem as well as an attitude problem, because he can't hold his booze the way he used to. I've left him a bit of money, enough for the hotel bill, but I didn't think it was good for him to have a lot – he'll only drink it all away, and what good will that be to anyone? I've also taken his passport because I reckon he's not going anywhere much at all. At all. I shall post the letter at the airport, and then go somewhere really exotic. I don't think I'll tell you where, Marshall, on account of I haven't entirely made up my mind. Also, though I've not done anything really awful, I expect that if people knew where I was they might come and make a nuisance of themselves. I might decide to sell my story to the press later on, if I run out of cash, but that's not going to be for a long, long time, I can assure you.

I wonder what you'll be doing when you get this letter. I imagine you'll still be lying in that boring bed in that boring hospital waiting to die. It really is a disgraceful place, by the way. Dr Z has been ripping it off for years. And bonking Amelia, but that's another story. And since I'm sending a copy of this letter to the Old Bill – aren't I organised, Marshall? – I should think they might be quite interested in having a gander at the accounts. Well, that's for them to worry about.

There's one more thing, Marshall, and I should think you're already feeling a bit aerated about this. Where are the Mauritius stamps? Well, you certainly deserve them after you took so much trouble to get hold of them, and you've probably seen them already. That is if you opened the envelope I shoved this tape in. I stuck them on the front along with the usual American ones which they told me I needed to send the letter airmail to England. I didn't quite know where to send the letter, but in the end I sent it to Jack's house, because I think Sylvia must be one of the most trustworthy people in the world. Jack thinks the world of your sister by the way. He often said he thought she was far too good for him (but that wouldn't be difficult, would it? Ha ha!). The stamps were the mint ones, you see, and they still had a bit of sticky left on them, which is astonishing after all those years, isn't it? But to be on the safe side I put a bit of glue on the back of them as well. I know you said they're worth a bit more mint than used, but they're so rare anyway, aren't they? And they will complete your marvellous collection, which is the main thing. You can soak them off the envelope, I know (well I suppose you can, but now I come to think about it, the Uhu might pose the odd problem or two). When I was with the nuns we used to soak stamps off envelopes and send them off to the missions to help all the poor people in the world. But it doesn't seem to have done much good, Marshall, does it, because there seem to be many more poor people than ever there used to be and I don't imagine that boxes and boxes of old stamps are quite what they're hoping for when the aid convoys rumble in. I've sent them some of your money; a tenth actually, because that's what it said to do in the Bible. Father Mulcahy back in Clare would be proud of me. Better than Jack spending it on booze is what I say. I'm sure you agree.

Must go now. They've just called my flight. Perhaps you could hear them. It's really great travelling first-class. You meet what Jack would call 'a really nice class of person'. I wonder if they would think of me as a really nice class of person. I've spent quite a bit on clothes and make-up and things, just the sort of things I'd have got if I'd won the Darlin' Girls from Clare comp., so I don't know that even my best friends would recognise me though I guess Fidelina would. Ha! You're probably my best friend now, Marshall. I really like you. Much more than Marcel, though he is such a poppet in bed. That must be why I've taken such a lot of trouble telling you all this. I thought you deserved it.

I'll sign off now before going through to the departure lounge and whatever fate has in store for little Stacey Anne. Lots of love – and to Sylvia too – and a long life.

The end of the recording was followed by a kiss, a moan of desire, and a chuckle. Sylvia screwed up the note and the envelope in which it and the tape had arrived, and hurled them into the waste-paper basket.

27

*T*here was a remission. It was sparked by anger.

'You stupid, *stupid* woman! Don't you realise what you've done? Don't you realise: What is it all *for*?'

'Stupid I may be, Marshall, but not so stupid as to give away all my money to an Irish whore.'

'I gave it to your husband.'

'Exactly. How stupid can you get?' Sylvia sat on the bed. 'Well frankly, Marshall, the whole situation is too melodramatic for words. And what are we going to *do*? What are we going to live on?'

Jeremy came to visit him in the late afternoon with a cup of tea.

'Can't stay long, I'm afraid. Ma's in a terrible state and Agnes is not much better. I try not to think about it all. Concentrate on homework. Revising the Second World War. Everyone kept making speeches. You're looking better, Uncle Marshall.'

'Your grandfather made some of the best. "Blood, sweat and tears", that was his. He tried it out, found it worked, and lent it to Churchill.'

'Fuckaduck!' said Jeremy with an endearing smile. 'Is that really true? Trouble is, I can't use it, can I? The examiners would think I'd made it up. The shortcomings of the examination system. They don't want the truth, just an acceptable version of it. A stands for "acceptable". Still it's nice to know that my grandad helped win the war. Even if my dad's a murderer.'

Marshall asked the boy to retrieve the crumpled envelope and gave him an acceptable version of what had taken place earlier in the day.

'If you put the envelope between two pieces of linen and iron it flat, it may improve things a bit.'

As soon as he had inserted the wrecked Mauritius stamps into their appropriate page, Marshall took Jeremy through his collection, country by precious country. Flattered to have the attention of someone who displayed genuine interest in the collection, Marshall spoke to Jeremy with such scholarly passion about the French imperforates, the Cape of Good Hope Woodblocks, that Jeremy was fired with excitement and demanded to know everything, not just about the stamps, but the conditions under which they had been acquired, the price Marshall had paid for them, the evidence for each being genuine.

Marshall was like a swimmer emerging from the water to take a gulp of air. The droplets shone on his shoulders, his eyes flashed in the sun. He sat up in bed; he sat on the side of the bed; he sat in a chair.

It was Jeremy who volunteered to take Marshall to the investiture, to push the chair, to see to the arrangements, to talk to the officials, to avoid disasters, to keep the conversation flowing.

'What are they knighting you *for*?' He found it odd to hold a conversation with someone sitting in front of him and facing in the same direction. If you wished to, you could make faces that did not at all suit the sentiments you were uttering. The same applied to the other party. Like actors in a poor soap opera.

'For being a good and obediently civil servant.'

'And were you?'

'Oh, by their own standards, I was superb. The standards are not high. It's probably more difficult being a good plumber than a good civil servant.'

'But they don't knight plumbers.'

'Only if they become very rich plumbers and give very sizeable sums to the government. They would have crashed the sword on to my shoulder years ago, Jeremy, if I hadn't had words with Sir Archie. Then he died, so, in the flicker of time between his dissolution and my own, they are completing unfinished business.'

'Will they actually do that thing? With the sword, I mean.'

'Tap it anyway, yes. It's called the accolade. In battle it was enough for the King, or just a nobleman, to clap you on the shoulder and say: "Be a knight." Your duty then was to defend Christendom against the infidel and in peacetime to appear at tourneys for the tourists.'

'They knight quite a lot of infidels now, don't they? And tourists.'

The ballroom was passionate with scarlet and gold. A band played selections from Gilbert and Sullivan, and four Gentleman Ushers scuttled around attending to the needs of, and giving detailed instructions to, the hundred or more recipients and their fan clubs. There were small creamy cakes with raspberries atop, and tea served in porcelain cups and saucers.

Jeremy said: 'I don't believe this. It's like a Walt Disney film. How can people take all this stuff seriously?'

There was a fanfare and the Queen entered, escorted by two Ghurka officers. There was a susurration in the eager and soon-to-be-honoured crowd. There was She and there were They and wasn't life extraordinary. In front of the dais the Queen was joined by five Yeomen of the Guard, and the Lord Chamberlain, whose party it officially was.

At much the same moment police officers were beating at the door of Sylvia's house in Bexleyheath. They were not the same men who had visited Marshall in the clinic. They were very senior. They explained to Sylvia that it was not really Marshall they had called to see. It was difficult to imagine that they had much of a case against him, and by the time they got all the papers together, he would not be in a fit state to undergo an interrogation, would he? They were more interested in finding out whether Sylvia had been in touch with Jack, and, when she insisted that she certainly had not been, advised her that an arrest was imminent, and that extradition would follow. If Jack contacted her what would she do? She said she had no idea. Aid and abet? She didn't understand what that meant. And her children? She said that they would have to answer for themselves. They looked weightily serious. She did realise, did she, that as the wife of a murder suspect, Sylvia's movements would be carefully monitored. However if she were prepared to co-operate with them, they could probably avoid most of the unpleasantnesses.

'It's not true, is it?' asked Sylvia, 'that stuff on the tape. You probably already know that the girl's a compulsive liar.'

'Two old ladies called Turnbull and a dog were found battered to death in Wakefield, madam. There's not a lot of arguing with that.'

'Yes, but the other things . . .'

The senior policemen glanced at each other then.

'According to the forensic reports there was no evidence of sexual molestation on either lady.'

Sylvia said: 'But if the girl was prepared to lie about that, she could just as well have lied about everything else. Jack's my husband. I know what he's capable of. He's not a bad man, only weak, as most of us are.'

'He's awaiting extradition. As soon as we've questioned him we'll know a good deal more. We would have done so already except for the little matter of expenses and cutbacks. Now may we have a word with your brother? He of course must have a vested interest in clearing this matter up. Is he upstairs?'

'Not just at the moment,' Sylvia replied with a touch of sisterly pride, 'he's at Buckingham Palace being knighted.'

The Gentleman Ushers were most awfully tactful and considerate.

'The procedures are quite lengthy,' they explained to Jeremy, 'and if your father, bearing in mind his state of health, would at any time like to jump the gun, just a word to us . . .'

'If you speak directly to me,' Marshall said, 'communications would be both speedier and more precise. For a start I am not the boy's father but his uncle. Next I am in no particular hurry to meet the Queen, having met her on several occasions in the past and having been kept waiting by Sir Archibald Munro for so many years, but I do have a special request. Would it be at all possible to visit the –'

'Gentlemen's? No problem, sir.'

'Stamp Room,' Marshall persisted.

The Ushers were not sure about that, and went off to seek a ruling, while Marshall explained to Jeremy about the Royal Stamp Collection, initiated by George V, and continued by monarchs ever since. There were no objections raised to Marshall's request and Jeremy pushed his uncle along encrusted corridors and through gilded doors. Eventually they were shown into a room with which Marshall was already familiar. It was the stamp room of his dreams. The Gentleman Usher who had accompanied them introduced them to an unusually shaped man with a dewlap and a paunch who shuffled around the room to meet them. He was, he told them with magisterial dignity, the Curator. He too Marshall had met before.

'Which countries are you most concerned about?' the Curator inquired. 'They are all here. I can take you from Greenland's icy mountains to Afric's rocky shores. Here, for example –' and he flicked a button which illuminated a display case '– are some stamps from the Autonomous Republic of Hatay, created after the Franco-Syrian Treaty of 1937. Tiresome stamps of no serious aesthetic interest to philatelists or historians or anyone, except perhaps those who had taken part in the accompanying riots. Her Majesty has never to my knowledge expressed any interest in the stamps of Hatay. It is conceivable that you are the first people, besides myself, ever to look upon these unexceptional scraps of paper. Quite uncommon though, and Her Majesty feels privileged, I'm sure, to know that they are part of the Royal Collection.'

The Curator had begun without enthusiasm but as he warmed to his task he showed Marshall and Jeremy some of the finest treasures in the Royal Collection. Where most collectors had single examples, here were corner blocks; where most had corner blocks, here were sheets. The condition of the stamps put Marshall's pristine ones to shame. The Curator wondered if there was any country – the collection was predictably strongest in the Commonwealth – which the visitors had a particular interest in seeing. Mauritius, said Marshall.

The Mauritius stamps were ravishing. To the Curator's astonishment and Jeremy's embarrassment Marshall burst into tears. He sobbed as if his heart was breaking, and then it did, for he died.

'I think I understand what happened,' said Jeremy to his mother and sister some hours later. 'He had wanted perfection and he risked everything to achieve it and ultimately he failed. Others achieved it without a struggle. In such circumstances what is the point of continuing?'

Sylvia, who had done a good deal of crying herself, failed to understand Jeremy's theory in any particular. Agnes however adopted it with enthusiasm.

'He's right. Jeremy's right. That's how people are. And that's just what we should be warned against. There'll *always* be others better than you at anything and everything. You have to lower your expectations. You have to be human.'

'He didn't even get his knighthood,' said Sylvia. 'That's sad too. I wonder if they give it to them posthumously.'

'People died for his stamps,' said Jeremy. 'Terrible things happened. And he asked me to try and iron out the creases. Well, I mean. They destroyed him.'

'We can right wrongs,' said Agnes splendidly. 'That's something the survivors can achieve.'

Sylvia looked cross rather than sad. 'I just don't know what you two are on about. My brother's not yet cold.' At which Agnes and Jeremy began to giggle and, after a while, so did Sylvia.

'I think I know what we can do to put things to rights,' said Agnes later that night. Her brother was impressed. They discussed her plan until late into the night, and then they put it to Sylvia, who had been making jam to stay awake. Sylvia thought long and hard and then, with great generosity, agreed.

28

*T*wo months after Marshall's death and within two days of each other, the sales of two great stamp collections took place in London: the Turnbull Collection and the Marshall Collection. The Turnbull was to be sold at Harmers, the Marshall just down the road at Phillips.

Arthur Winepress had told Sylvia of Marshall's desire that his first issue collection should be put on permanent display, but this desire had not been formalised and it was up to Sylvia, as Marshall's only beneficiary, to do as she thought best. She had said:

'Sell the beastly things. All of them.'

Harry Nissen met Marcel at the Phillips viewing. It was a slow business. So much interest had been excited by the sale of Marshall's stamps that those who arrived early stayed late. Those who did not arrive early never gained admittance to the viewing room at all. But both Marcel and Harry had requested to view the collection privately before the hordes rampaged in; and, being regular and reliable clients, they were admitted on the Friday of the previous week.

'Have you viewed at Harmers yet?' Harry wanted to know. Marcel said that he had. 'Notice anything the two collections have in common?' Marcel said that he didn't understand what Harry was getting at. 'Both are remarkably authentic. Until you turn to Mauritius. Then you find that the Turnbull Collection has the Post Office set in poor facsimiles, while the Marshall Collection has got the authentic set, but they are in dire condition and stuck to a contemporary cover. The only stamps in the whole scintillating lot which are less than very fine.'

'What are you bidding for?' asked Marcel – the age-old question of one stamp dealer to another.

'A bit of this and a bit of that. A few gaps to fill and a few clients to satisfy. And you?'

'Tasmania and some of the Canal Zone,' said the Frenchman, who was chiefly interested in the German States.

'Sad to see a collection like this broken up. But Marshall was a sour old devil; never seemed to take much pleasure in them at all. Still, I suppose the component parts will go towards some other great collections.'

'As ours do, my friend when we die,' said Marcel.

Judas and Celia looked in too.

'I owe him a good deal,' said Judas. 'Including an annual increment.'

'You get it up once a year?' Celia had been offered a job running Sotheby's Pulborough operation and felt relieved of the burden of courtesy. 'I wonder, though, was there anything left when Marshall died?'

'Not so much quantity as quality,' said Judas. 'One or two treasures which he'd kept back for a rainy day. A Fabergé ink-well I recall that was exquisite.'

'You never mentioned it till now.'

'You never asked.'

'So why did you conceal it from me?'

'Not conceal really. There was so much we never spoke of. Besides which, *ma petite*, I thought you might not approve.'

'Of what, precisely?'

There were some shushes from the philatelists who were huddled like figures from a Chinese terracotta army over their desiderata.

'I had a word with Jane, the housemaid, then I had a word with the bailiffs. You didn't know about the bailiffs? Fancy it coming to that! Anyway, the thing is that I bought the remaining chattels from them for a considerable sum.'

'Considerable?'

'Considerable to them; derisory to me.'

'Not only did you never mention them but they never turned up at auction. Certainly no Fabergé ink-well did.'

'But of course not. I had no authority to sell.'

Celia was dumbfounded. She detested the man, but could not avoid admiring him.

'You scum-bag!' The terracotta army indicated further disapproval. 'Well he is!' Celia added and made her getaway. She had a new lover, a footballer. He was tremendously jealous and yet coltishly anxious to please. He was a striker, he said, with a great left foot. Celia told him she quite believed it.

29

In a small and modestly furnished flat in Tel Aviv there lived a woman, born in Germany, a survivor of the Holocaust, now a naturalised Israeli citizen. She wore her grey hair swept back from her forehead in the sensible style favoured by Golda Meir. She had no living relatives and her experiences in Ravensbrück had rendered her sterile. None the less she found that even in late middle age there were pleasures to be enjoyed: neighbours who took it upon themselves to share an occasional social evening with her; books, which she read avidly, especially books on geology, in which she was expert and about which she lectured at the university. And music, especially Bruckner, in which she delighted.

The anticipated arrival of Agnes and Jeremy had perplexed Miss Auerbach and caused her such anxiety that she had found difficulty in sleeping. She resorted to sleeping pills; otherwise dreams of the past haunted her in her brief moments of slumber.

But these are merely children, she thought, as she ushered them in. What can they have to do with me? Elderly people who have established a useful routine welcome the irruption of the past as little as the imminence of the future. However, curiosity is a powerful motivator and so she served them falafel and coffee so thick and dark that it coated the tongue.

Agnes and Jeremy were also nervous and by no means convinced that they were doing the right – or the sensible – thing. The morning after she had received the approval of her mother and brother to the scheme, Agnes had bought two tickets to Tel Aviv, buying singles because they were all she could then afford.

Jeremy had taken charge of the attaché case, the same one with which Marshall had set out to Wakefield, and had managed to sneak it through customs without dreary formalities, though Agnes had secured the necessary papers. In return it was agreed that Agnes would do the talking.

She did. Miss Auerbach's English was heavily accented but she understood a good deal. Enough anyway. She understood that the English children had brought with them a large sum of money, raised at some auction, and that they were claiming that some of it belonged to her father and now therefore belonged to her.

'We couldn't trace the others,' Agnes concluded, 'but we know the bronzes were your father's. Will you accept what we have for you and help us to distribute the rest?'

'I was on a ship that out of Hamburg sailed. It to the port of Jaffa came and all of us on the board – for we were very many and sad – shouted for joy the Promised Land to see. There were British with soldiers on the dock – but yet it was already peacetime – who waved at us no, to go away, no, no. We must not to land. We must go to home. Home? we asked. What is that if not this? I did not understand then. I do not understand now. Why did they not us to land permit? Why this money you bring here? Go away, kinde. What is it with you British? You go to home now.'

When they tried to persuade her she became angry and tearful. Finally Agnes said to let them at least give her a present. No, she said, no present. Presents were from friends.

In their comfortable American-owned hotel they discussed what best to do.

'We are out of our class,' said Agnes. 'it was a crazy idea anyway.'

'All the best ideas are crazy. So do we just go home?'

'I'll tell you what I think. Let me complete my psychology degree and then I'll come back here with the money. But I'll talk to people who know about such things. Maybe there's a charity for victims of the Holocaust. Maybe we can turn up some of the other names. Maybe I'll even talk to Dad. I don't know.'

'The money isn't ours,' said Jeremy. 'And Miss Auerbach doesn't want it. And while we had a licence to bring it into Israel we may have problems getting it out. It's a real downer.'

'It's a bugger. But it shouldn't damage us psychologically. That's what the textbooks say. That will have happened a long time ago.'

'I don't feel damaged,' said Jeremy, slumped on his bed and looking tired, 'but I do feel frustrated.'

Later they talked for the first time about their father and the murders. Agnes sat beside Jeremy, put her arm around him, and said that Sylvia would need all the help they could give her, and Jack too, but that, when all was said and done, they had their own lives to lead. That was what really mattered. But Jeremy was asleep.

Well, well, well, thought Agnes, the textbooks don't tell the half of it. Here am I in a Tel Aviv hotel for no very clear purpose with my brother asleep beside me and a very large amount of money in cash at the foot of the bed. My father is to go on trial for murder, and my mother seems to have become entirely reactive. Awful things have happened and we seem to be unscathed. She looked at her hand against the moonlight. It was the hand of a child. Then she too, tired of brooding about abstractions, fell asleep, and thought that she had met Marshall in a large smoke-filled waiting room. A catechism ensued.

'Where are we?'

'Nowhere much, Agnes.'

'What are we doing here?'

'I'm dead. You're a tourist.'

'What's it like being dead.'

'Like being asleep.'

'I'm asleep.'

'I know.'

A pause. Then:

'Is it really you, Uncle Marshall?'

'Yes.'

'Will I remember you when I wake up?'

'No.'

'I won't remember any of this?'

'None of it.'

'What should I do? Surely you can tell me.'

'Your confusion will last some months. Then you will know. What you will do will help your mother. I should have. I was looking for perfection. How childish.'

'Are you sad to have left us behind?'

'It fades. The mind grows easier. I was sad when the stamps were sold.'

'Is there a God?'

'What do you think?'

'Is there a heaven and hell?'

'Of course not.'

'So what happens in the end?'

'Read on.'